WHITELEY WORLDS
ISSUE 39

CONNOR WHITELEY

No part of this book may be reproduced in any form or by any electronic or mechanical means. Including information storage, and retrieval systems, without written permission from the author except for the use of brief quotations in a book review.

This book is NOT legal, professional, medical, financial or any type of official advice.

Any questions about the book, rights licensing, or to contact the author, please email
connorwhiteley@connorwhiteley.net

Copyright © 2024 CONNOR WHITELEY

All rights reserved.

INTRODUCTION

I know I say this every year but one October, I really need to do a Halloween or "darker" issue of Whiteley Worlds. Even though I know I will never remember to do that and there are some Halloween-ish elements of this issue anyway.

In addition, as the editor of this magazine, I don't like planning out that far ahead that I would need to write specific content for a specific issue. I am more than happy to do that for a collection, a Kickstarter Make 100 project or any other type of fiction project. Yet writing specific content for an issue of Whiteley Worlds just seems flat out wrong to me.

I don't know why but it just does.

Anyway, as we head towards the fun and spooky time of year called Halloween, you'll be able to escape into another insanely fun, enthralling and gripping issue of Whiteley Worlds through 5 different unputdownable short stories and two stellar novellas.

We kick off this issue with a wonderfully heartwarming, romantic and sweet gay romance short story, *Love and Trains Through The Years*. If you enjoy sweet holiday romances then this is a brilliant short story providing the perfect escape as the nights grow darker.

Our second story is the complete opposite of a sweet romance yet it is still gripping, enthralling and perfect escapism. *Freedom Day* shows the hardboiled side of Christmas with a grumpy former detective in a wrecked pub when disaster strikes. If you enjoy hardboiled fiction then you don't want to miss this story.

Now for our third story in this issue, it is very rare that I write historical fiction. Personally, I don't really like historical fiction and I find it very hard to read. I flat out cannot read Regency fiction because I have tried so hard to enjoy it but it is not to my reader tastes. Yet one area of historical fiction I love to read is World War Two historical fiction, more specifically French resistance or spy fiction.

I've written a fair few World War Two spy stories before, and whilst *Won't Be Home For Christmas* doesn't feature any spies, it is still a heartwarming, lovely and emotional short story about love, family and war. If you enjoy historical fiction then you're in for a treat.

So far in this issue, we've had romantic and light, hardboiled and potentially heartbreaking stories, but our fourth story taps into the fantasy elements which is perfect for this time of year.

Feast of Drunkenness comes from my interest in ancient holidays and if memory serves me, the ancient Egyptians had a feast of drunkenness where they would celebrate how one of their gods tricked Apex (the God of Death and Chaos) into a barrel of red wine to defeat him. That's the general gist of the holiday so this holiday-themed story bounces off that in a very usual and modern way.

Finally, we wrap up all these brilliant short stories with the gripping, unputdownable and gut-wrenching holiday short story *Poisoning The Winter Village Contest*. I won't give too much away about this Christmas story but it is a fun short story about revenge, laughter and justice.

A perfect holiday crime story to escape the long dark nights.

Furthermore, we have two stellar novellas debuting in these pages this month. First up, we have the suspenseful, spellbinding, edge-of-your-seat adventure *Murder*. I know I don't normally add the blurbs but it serves as a good introduction to this magical book:

When Lady Ithane Tano barely survives the annihilation of her empire, she must hunt down those responsible. Set in a rich, exciting, vivid fantasy world, Connor Whiteley masterfully writes a gripping story about love, hope and friendship against an awe-inspiring backdrop of an ever-darkening world.

From its tense beginning to deepening mystery to stellar conclusion, Connor Whiteley takes readers on an enthralling fantasy journey in this new addition to the powerful series.

READ NOW!

Lastly, everyone's favourite private investigator Bettie English returns in this issue with another gripping, race against time mystery. In *Eight Hours*, Bettie English and team only have 8 hours to find evidence to arrest a killer before he escapes forever. With a heartbroken mother, justice and future potential victims' lives on the line, Bettie knows she can't afford to fail.

Now we know all the exciting stories in this issue, let's turn over the page and start exploring some Whiteley Worlds.

AVAILABLE AT ALL MAJOR BOOKSELLERS!

AVAILABLE AT ALL MAJOR BOOKSELLERS!

LOVE AND TRAINS THROUGH THE YEARS
A Gay Contemporary Holiday Romance Short Story

LOVE AND TRAINS THROUGH THE YEARS

I, Gabriel Darling, had always flat out loved the wonderfully modern, comfortable and red fabric seats of the train from London St Pancras near where I went to university to Newcastle up North. There was free Wi-Fi, which was always brilliant, and compared to other trains in the UK, this one was just so modern and great in ways that a lot of other trains simply weren't.

I was sitting near the very back of the train when it happened, I had met the love of my life (not that I actually knew it back then). I was sitting next to the massive window that these sort of trains had, and I was people-watching to see who was on the platform. There were so many fit businessmen and women in their black dresses and suits as they rushed towards their trains. They all probably wanted to make it home for Christmas, something that was only a few days away.

There was a particular family that caught my eye. It was a man in a business suit, a wife in a very thin dress that wasn't cut out for December at all and two young daughters in matching Christmas jumpers. Not that either one looked happy to be wearing it. They just looked so bright and happy compared to the cold, wintry grey of the train platform.

Something jerked me in my delightful soft seat and I weakly smiled as more and more people of all different shapes, sizes and heights walked past me to get to their seats. It was a shame a bunch of them were banging their suitcases against the back of my seat as they placed them on the rack, but that was life and I was just looking forward to finally going home.

I would get to see my mum, dad and my brothers. Their girlfriends might even turn up, which they probably would because me and my parents were starting to doubt my brothers actually had girlfriends. They always spoke about them but we never saw them.

The sweet aromas of chestnuts, cloves and mulled wine filled my senses as a bottle of something was cracked open by the people in front of me. The laughs that came from them were definitely female and I was just glad everyone was enjoying the holiday season.

I went to reach down to grab my large science fiction book that I was working my way through when I saw someone was looking at me out of the corner of my eye.

"Excuse me?" the man asked.

I almost shivered at the sound of the man's deep, manly, velvety voice. It was so intense and so great that I really wanted to hear his voice again and again.

When I looked up, it took everything I had not to cum right there and then. I was looking at the most beautiful man I had ever seen. My body shook slightly and as much as I wanted it to stop I just couldn't.

The man was solid, short and seriously fit. He didn't have any muscles, he didn't workout but he was as thin as a rake and he was just stunning. The way his longish brown hair flowed was beautiful and his youngish, boyish grin was just striking.

He was a stunner and I was really hoping he was going to be sitting next to me for the next four hours.

"Did you go to University College London?" the hottie asked. "You take English Literature, right?"

I cocked my head. "Yes, why do you want to know?"

"Oh sorry, I guess that sounds a bit weird. I thought I recognised you. I do Classics and your lecture is right next to mine on a Monday and I thought I had seen you a few times. You're a little hard to miss. I'm Thomas by the way,"

I grinned and I gestured the man to take a seat. I flat out loved it as he sat down next to me, I got a delightful whiff of his manly musk and some spicy clove scented aftershave. I was really going to enjoy these next few hours.

And that was what happened.

For the next four hours, we spoke constantly and we learnt everything there was about each other. I learnt he was a stunningly hot man that loved classical history, literature and really understanding the past. Originally I had doubted the Classics could ever be important and they were just for university students that didn't want a proper degree.

But it turned out I was completely wrong. Or at least Thomas had such a passionate and interesting way of talking about his subject that

I was hooked on every beautiful word that poured out of his mouth.

And it was interesting when he was asking me questions about my degree. We both agreed that English Literature degrees were useless because I had no intention of going into teaching and my degree wasn't exactly what I thought it was going to be about, so I was changing to Classic History to be honest.

Again, not exactly useful but it was interesting and my dad worked at a major Northern museum so I did sort of have a job at the end of it.

When my train pulled into Newcastle, we had exchanged phone numbers, wished each other a happy Christmas and I had almost kissed him but we hadn't. He was still the most beautiful man I had ever seen and for the next two days I couldn't stop thinking about him.

Then it was Christmas, me and my family had visited some family in France over New Year's and I had loved the winter break. And when the university term started again, my lectures had moved and I never ever saw that cutie, beautiful man for the rest of the year. I had texted him of course but he had never ever replied.

The next Christmas I was thankfully sitting up near the front of the train and I didn't have any of those annoying people banging their suitcases into the back of my seat. But I actually would have preferred that because this year I had two little kids (boys obviously) who were kicking the back of my seat constantly. The mother had already threatened to cancel Christmas for them, she had apologised time and time again but she was a single mother and when it looked she was about to cry, I had hugged her and told her it was okay.

It wasn't, but it was nearly Christmas so I didn't want her any more stressed than she already was.

Besides from the constant kicking of the two kids, it was a nice enough train and it was a shame I didn't have a window seat but I didn't mind too much. The train smelt of grapefruit, lemons and limes from the cleaning chemicals and I was just about to open a nonfiction book on Ancient Rome when I saw someone out of the corner of my eye.

"Hello again Gabriel," Thomas said.

I frowned and I looked up at him. He was still so beautiful, so stunning and he looked exactly the same as last year which was perfect. My body shook slightly. My heart rate increased. My mouth went dry but I was still annoyed at him.

He sat down without permission. "I'm sorry I never replied. It wasn't that I don't like you, I really do, it's just I don't know how these things work,"

I could only nod as I enjoyed his sweet fruity aftershave that was overwhelming my nose in a very, very good way. And I wanted to see where he took this conversation.

"I know you probably think I always get guys and hit on but I don't. I only came out a week after I met you and that went great, but I was still learning how all this gay dating works," Thomas said grinning.

"And when you did figure it out," I said wanting to just start talking normally with him.

"I don't know. The university term started up, I went to a lot of queer events and you were never there. I got deadlines, assignments and I forgot to text you,"

I wanted to hug him as he looked at the floor like he had committed some kind of crime, and maybe he had to be honest, maybe he had committed a crime against my heart. I had texted him, I had wanted to go slow and I had shown a lot of interest. I hadn't even dated this entire year because of him and that was bad.

I had basically put my heart on the line for him this year and he hadn't even been bothered to text me.

The train jerked as it left the station and I just hugged Thomas and felt something hard press against my leg.

"How about we just talk now?" I asked enjoying the sweet fruitiness of his aftershave. "And we can get to know each other like we would have through texting,"

"I would really like that Gabriel,"

I grinned like a little schoolboy as that is exactly what we did for the next four hours. It turned out that Thomas had had an even more interesting childhood than I did in terms of being gay. My family had always been supportive, loving and encouraging as hell towards me being gay and whatnot. Whereas Thomas's family had never ever been homophobic, they were hardly vocal allies and Thomas had never really felt great enough to come out, so that was exactly what the past year had been all about.

Thomas had been exploring, learning and just seeing the sort of gay person he wanted to be. He didn't like being with the stereotypical gays because that wasn't him. He also didn't like hanging out with the partying gays because he wasn't a partying or clubbing person, but I was really happy that he had found some friends with the nerdy gays and I had laughed about that a lot ever since.

Yet I was a little surprised that Thomas hadn't kissed, had sex or done anything with a guy except hugging them and even holding a hand in public. Which was probably a much bigger deal to him than it was to me because I've been doing it for close to a decade.

"What do you think?" Thomas asked as we both sipped some sweet, piping hot lattes that we had both ordered.

And I was surprised at myself as I replied because I was actually proud of him and I felt amazing for him. I had never felt so happy, so proud and so excited for another person in all my life. I was sitting next to a beautifully hot, sexy man that was just starting to learn how amazing being gay could be.

I was so excited for all the things he was going to realise in the future. He was going to experience how amazing kissing another man was, how sensational gay sex was and how lovely just being in a relationship with another man was. He was going to be happy so happy and oddly enough, that made me so damn happy in return.

And that was how I knew, I just knew that I was seriously falling for beautiful Thomas. We had spoken for 8 hours straight basically and there wasn't an awkward moment, a silence or anything to be honest. It was just a wonderful conversation that I didn't like to end as we pulled into Newcastle Station and I hopped off and he continued towards his home.

But this time he texted me over and over.

That particular Christmas had to be one of the weirdest Christmases ever because I flat out loved spending time with my family, seeing my family in France and just enjoying my time back in Newcastle. But I also felt fantastic because every single day without fail, I was texting a beautiful man that was really into me.

We spoke about our Christmases, our presents and our lives. And we even made plans together once we got back to London, and we did those plans to the letter and we loved every minute of it.

I basically moved in with him straight away once we were back, I was fast friends with his three flatmates, we laughed and spent a lot of nights together. I showed Thomas all the wonderful delights that being gay brought a person, both the social and the adult benefits, and we had even gone on a few trips together to France.

My family flat out loved Thomas from the moment they met him, and I couldn't blame them.

The next Christmas, as the train went smoothly along going towards Newcastle because beautiful Thomas was staying at mine this Christmas and then we were going to his for New Year. We had spoken for three hours straight and then Thomas had fallen asleep and I was just hugging him. I had my face buried in his neck as he slept and I enjoyed the wonderful feminine aftershave that I had brought him as a little present for myself as much as it was for him.

And I couldn't believe how lucky I was, because I had a boyfriend I basically loved at this point, I was living my best life and I was so looking forward to this Christmas and all the Christmases after that. We might have met on a train and fallen in love because we met on a train at Christmas but our love was a lot deeper than that.

A type of passionate, wonderful love that made me feel warm, light and incredible. Something I had never experienced before but I was so excited to keep feeling it whenever I saw beautiful Thomas. Something I was going to keep doing through the years, because I really did love him and he really loved me too.

AVAILABLE AT ALL MAJOR BOOKSELLERS!

AUTHOR OF BETTIE ENGLISH PRIVATE EYE MYSTERIES
CONNOR WHITELEY
FREEDOM
DAY
A HARDBOILED DETECTIVE FICTION HOLIDAY MYSTERY SHORT STORY

FREEDOM DAY

A Hardboiled Detective Fiction Holiday Mystery Short Story

Some people might have gotten excited about Christmas, New Year and a whole bunch of other so-called great holidays in December, but I didn't. It wasn't that I didn't like those holidays but after a few years of them with three screaming kids, a lot of noisy neighbours and a lot of rubbish presents from horrible, posh in-laws you really start to develop a minor hatred of those holidays.

But there was one holiday I enjoyed. Yet even that was stretching that little positive word a little more than I would like to.

And that was Freedom Day, the last Sunday before Christmas when all our wives and girlfriends took out the children and grandchildren allowing us men to enjoy our time away from Christmas shopping. We were free to do whatever we wanted so all of us came to the pub and we certainly enjoyed it here.

I sat in my favourite wooden chair with lots of small wooden nobs pressing like daggers into my skin, at the best pub in the entire world. A lot of people might have said *Dave's Shack* was a shithole and they would be right. The pub wasn't anything that special and that was exactly how I liked it. I had always liked the beer-stained brown walls that had certainly seen better days and some of the walls had been eaten away by woodworm.

I don't know why Dave, the short little owner with a bald head, even bothered patching up the holes to the icy cold outside world. I rather liked the draft in the evening, especially when Dave's faulty gas fire started smoking and no one really cared.

The place was certainly a fire hazard but that was just part of its charm.

The entire shack smelt of cheap, watery alcohol with hints of whiskey, bourbon and moonshine making me really want to get on the good stuff. But it was a shame that Dave only allowed his friends and *best* customers to have access to them.

I was close to making the list but I wasn't good enough yet sadly.

Over the talking, muttering and moaning of the other regulars that were all middle-aged men like me and elderly men, I could sadly hear the damn roar of the boy racers zooming up the road outside.

This was a shithole in a bad area and I hated the boy racers for sure. The Shack itself was stuck in-between a collapsing building that used to be a high-rise office building and a petrol station that was smashed up more often than not.

I didn't mind it though because it kept the positive people out of it. This was a pub for the working man, the working class and it wasn't about to become trendy or do any rubbish like that.

"Ready for Freedom Day everyone?" Dave asked as he came in with a trolley full of beer for us.

I raised my cheap pint to cheers him and then I placed it back on the stained, slimy round wooden table in front of me. I noticed an elderly man was frowning at me and he looked awful in his holey green jumper and his face was a mixture of scars and broken jaws and noses, but I just waved him away.

"Can someone help me?" a woman asked.

The entire pub fell silent as I looked round to look at the small young woman who was standing in the rotting doorway of the pub. She was letting all the icy coldness of the horrible world outside into the pub and all the elderly men were moaning at her.

She was somewhat pretty but she was all bones and skin and model-like qualities. She wasn't a real woman but she looked like she needed help. I could see the fear in her young, innocent eyes and she was shaking in the doorway.

"Shut the damn door," an elderly man said.

"Come and sit over here love," I said to her and waved her over.

I didn't want to help her but even I wanted to know what a pretty young thing like her was doing in this sort of place. Young people didn't come to the Shack ever, maybe she was lost and if that was the case then I was going to give her directions and I was going to forget about her.

Today was Freedom Day and no one was

going to mess it up for me.

As the young woman sat down on the wooden chair opposite me, her eyes widened as she realised how sticky, cold and awful the chair was. Yeah, she definitely didn't belong here but she made herself sit down and that was a good sign.

"I hear you were a cop before you became this drunk," the young woman said. "My name is Jade by the way,"

"By the way I didn't ask," I said disgusted she dared to call me a drunk. "I was a cop but the justice system is just rubbish. I tried fighting the good fight to try to get criminals rehabilitated so they wouldn't reoffend but that doesn't make the police look good apparently. Bullshit is what I say,"

I took a sip of my beer as I was surprised I was still as passionate for that work as I had been a decade ago when I gave it all up.

"That's why I came to find you," Jade said placing one of my ancient business cards on my left knee.

"I'm impressed," I said leaning forward. "What you want here?"

"I want you to deal with my husband," Jade said as she rubbed her cheeks and revealed black bruises and cuts to her face.

"Jesus," I said and I had to fight the urge to go into police mode. I wanted to tell her to call the cops, fill out a statement and so on but I couldn't.

The justice system didn't work for abuse victims. It was always critical that people came forward so I would make Jade do that later but I needed to do something to help her now.

The sooner I helped her the sooner she would leave and I could enjoy Freedom Day.

"Where's my wife?" a man asked storming into the pub and pounded his fist on the bar where Dave was working.

I looked over and grinned at the man standing there. Jade certainly knew how to pick the idiots. This man was all muscles with large tattoos belonging to more gangs than I cared to admit. His nose had clearly been broken in a ton of fights but somehow this awful man managed to make it work on him.

He looked somewhat good but I had to deal with him and help Jade.

My hands formed fists as Jade got smaller and she curled herself up into a ball. It was probably more out of instinct than anything else.

I took another sip of my beer and stood up.

"You," I said clicking my fingers. "You need to get out of here and leave your wife alone,"

"I'm ain't leaving until I get my wife back you punk," he said.

I just grinned because I had never been called a punk before, that was a new one.

The man came over to me and I placed myself firmly in-between him and Jade. There was no way in hell I was letting him anywhere near her.

"I will kill you bitch," he said.

"Leave me alone Derick. I want a divorce," Jade said.

Derick looked at me. "Get out the way or I will beat your sorry ass into the ground,"

I noticed the other regulars were on their feet now but I subtly shook my head. As much as I didn't really care about the elderly and middle-aged men here I didn't want them to get injured or whatnot. I still needed them as drinking buddies even if I wasn't allowed the real alcohol just yet.

I couldn't have them beating up Derick. I had to deal with him myself.

I picked up my beer. I threw it over him.

I hated wasting the precious piss poor liquid but if I was going to waste precious alcohol then now was the time to do it.

"You're going to regret that," Derick said breaking out into a fighting stance.

It only hit me then how stupid I had been. I had to protect Jade but Derick probably had three times the muscle I did and he was probably a street fighter for a living or he beat people up for cash.

I couldn't beat him in a fight but maybe I could beat him on skill.

He swung a fist at me.

I dodged.

He swung again.

Again.

I dodged both times.

I looked subtly behind me and smiled as Dave had turned on the gas fire that was roaring, splattering and pumping small amounts of black smoke.

Derick charged at me.

I leapt to one side.

Making sure to kick his ankles as he went past me.

He tripped. He hissed. He fell through the air.

I pushed him even harder.

Derick hissed in pain as he smashed his head into the gas fire. His clothes caught alight and he screamed louder and louder.

Jade rushed over with a large glass of clear liquid. She threw it over her husband.

It was moonshine.

Derick screamed in utter agony as the fire got even worse and he ran as fast as he could out of the pub. I knew he was going to die but this neighbourhood was such a shithole I doubted the cops would ever investigate.

Everyone was deadly silent in the pub so I just looked at Dave. "Two yellow pints please Davey boy,"

I was surprised when everyone was still silent and all the regulars just looked at Dave and nodded at him. Dave smiled and I couldn't believe what was happening the other regulars wanted me to be added to the list.

I was finally going to get real, beautiful alcohol in his place so Dave brought me over a small glass of bourbon that burnt like hell as I drank it. But I liked it all the same and as Dave got new drinks for the others, I coughed as the black smoke got a little worse.

"You okay?" I asked Jade as I sat back down on the slimy, sticky wooden chair.

"No," Jade said. "I just killed my husband and I have no friends, no family, no nothing. I'm all alone,"

I rolled my eyes. I had always hated working abuse cases because the damn criminals were always clever about isolating their victims. It was always down to other people to help them get back on their feet.

"You don't want me to be here," Jade said smiling. "I don't want to be here either,"

I rolled my eyes. "This place is a shithole but I think Dave would let you stay here for a night or two. Then go to a shelter, go to the police station and tell them what happened. They won't investigate. Derick is worthless,"

She nodded. "Will the shelters help me?"

"Yeah," I said knowing it was the truth. "It's funny really because today's Freedom Day in the pub. Normally it's freedom from our wives and our fatherly and husbandly duties, but maybe Freedom Day is actually about giving you your freedom to do whatever you want with your life,"

Jade nodded her thanks to Dave as he gave her a whiskey (the damn woman got on the list months before I did) and he passed me another fiery bourbon, and me and Jade cheered each other.

Then for the rest of the night, we laughed, talked and complained about how shit this neighbourhood was. And I never saw her again, I didn't really care because I knew she was okay, she was out living and she was enjoying her chance at being free and experiencing what true freedom was like.

I still go to the shithole Shack and nothing changes. I still like it, I still drink the real alcohol and I even talk to some of the regulars. It isn't much of a life but Freedom Day and all the other days of the year in the pub are still brilliant and I wouldn't change my life for anything.

"Another bourbon please Davey boy,"

AVAILABLE AT ALL MAJOR BOOKSELLERS!

WON'T BE HOME FOR CHRISTMAS
A World War Two Historical Fiction Short Story

3rd September 1939

Mary Woods was hardly surprised at the news the UK was going to war as she stood at her little metal kitchen sink as she tried to wash metal plates and mugs and cutlery from her breakfast in the icy cold water. The entire kitchen was as clean as she could keep it but the small wooden table and wooden green cabinets were so old that they just seemed to attract the dirt.

Mary had tried to keep the cabinets as clean as she could and she had broken all her nails trying to clean them, but they weren't going to be cleaned. It was just like the rest of their little house.

Mary normally loved cleaning the cream carpet in the living room, dining room and bedrooms but after the news on the wireless, she really hadn't felt like cleaning much of anything. Because what was the point of cleaning when her wonderful soldier husband Richard was going to be sent off to war?

The early afternoon air was cold with hints of pine, oak and smoke scenting it and it felt the strange taste of smoked bacon on her tongue, but Mary's stomach churned with worry about the declaration of war. She just wanted to know what would happen to her husband.

At least the white kitchen tiles were clean, Richard would like that when he came home, he always did like the house nice and tidy when he arrived. Mary was so excited to see her husband again and it would be great to hear him be pleased at her housekeeping efforts.

And it would be simply wonderful to have Richard back home so he could see little baby Liebert grow more and grow. Mary just loved her daughter than more anything else in the entire world.

Liebert was just such a cute little baby with large cheeks, tiny little fingers and the cutest laugh Mary had ever heard.

Baby Liebert was sleeping thankfully in front of the fire and Mary was glad to finally have it working. It had been tough without Richard here to provide the money for the food, heating and the mortgage that was going up and up each year. But that was why she married a soldier, because they were the best and it was always right and proper to die for one's country.

Of course that was a lie but Mary would never ever dare to admit that to Richard. He loved King and country far too much and he would probably laugh at Mary for being a stupid woman, but Mary wasn't stupid.

During the Great War, she had tried to help out the war effort as much as she could, she had worked a little for MI6 up in London and then when the war ended she had moved out of the city and met Richard when he first enlisted. He was so charming, wonderful and caring but he wasn't tolerant when people questioned the military.

He was even less tolerant when Mary mentioned how her three brothers had died during the Great War.

The letterbox opened and shut.

Mary just gave up on doing the dishes and went through the small cosy living room and checked on baby Liebert who was still peacefully sleeping and then she went to the front door and picked up the post that was on the off-cream carpet.

There was just some more bills and a letter in Richard's rough handwriting so Mary opened it and her life changed.

Richard wasn't coming home for ages because he had been given new orders and he was going to the frontline against Germany.

He promised Mary that he would be home for Christmas and the war would all be over but Mary was far from stupid.

She had heard the same rubbish in 1914 and she just knew that she wasn't going to see her amazing husband for ages if ever.

Mary was about to leave and check on Liebert again when the sound of young children outside made Mary's heart jump into her throat because the first evacuees of the village had arrived.

The war was real.

***

25th December 1939

After three long months of fighting, dying and killing, Mary wasn't exactly sure where her husband was as she sat around her little kitchen table at night. Mary had covered all the windows with black paper to make sure the damn Nazis couldn't see the light of the little candle she had in front of her.

The little metal kitchen sink was empty of all the pots and pans and plates from today, and it was amazing to see that little Liebert had loved her first small Christmas dinner. She really loved turkey which surprised Mary because normally her precious little girl was fussy about meat.

Mary had already given little Liebert her Christmas dinner, a little bath and she had read her a story before bedtime. That was ages ago and now Mary was alone like she always was these days.

As Mary sat in the cold darkness of the kitchen with it being so cold that Mary couldn't see her green cabinets or white tiled floor, Mary couldn't believe that she hadn't heard anything from the military or Richard.

It had been three months and not a single word from him. Her husband could be alive, a deserter or dead and she wouldn't have known.

That was annoying as hell but it was the unfortunate world she lived in.

In the daytime Mary made sure to drop off Liebert at the village's nanny that thankfully did all the childcare for free because she was retired and a wonderful woman. Then Mary went to her new job at the local post office but that was just depressing with all the war news that flowed in and out of the post office, and then Mary even made some jam with whatever she could afford at the local market then she sold it on.

Mary was just glad she would have enough money to live on for now and support a beautiful daughter.

The night was an icy cold one and normally when Richard was about the two of them would cuddle up under a blanket to keep warm but she couldn't do that this year. She had given Liebert all the blankets, pillows and everything else Mary could give her to make sure her little daughter didn't freeze.

It wouldn't be too long until Mary slept with Liebert so they could keep each other warm and that was a good way to save on heating. That was exactly what Mary needed to do right now because she had read all the newspaper reports about the bombings and air raids in London and the surrounding villages.

So what happened when the post office here was finally bombed? Mary didn't want to be out of a job and without any money.

Mary just had to try and save as much as she possibly could in the good times so hopefully she didn't have to starve when the bad times came.

But whatever happened Mary would protect her beautiful little girl no matter what.

***

25th December 1940

"That was wonderful Miss Mary,"

Mary weakly smiled at the vicar in his black church clothes as Mary, Liebert who could thankfully sit in a grown-up chair and the vicar sat around Mary's small wooden table. The wooden table was starting to fall apart sadly and she had had to cut out tons of woodworm last night but it was all she could afford.

It was still early afternoon so she didn't need to put up the black paper yet, the fire was thankfully roaring away in the living room that warmed up the entire house and thankfully the vicar had been kind enough to Mary to give her his rations of butter and fruit for the week so she could make a Christmas pudding.

The vicar had loved it and Mary still loved it that the house smelt so wonderful of fruit, sugar and cake. It had been so long since she had smelt the heavenly concoction that she had actually thought it was gas or something at first.

The three of them had their little chipped bowls in front of them that were all empty and Mary just watched the Vicar talk to Liebert. Mary wasn't religious in the slightest because surely a real God wouldn't allow such mass murder and wars to occur but she needed a friend.

Mary had needed the Vicar's help straight after the post office had been bombed, Mary was out of a job and there were so few businesses left in the village so she couldn't get another job. She had enough money to keep going for a little while but not long enough.

The Vicar had contacted her and wanted to give her the donations from the church that week, Mary said no because that money was for God's so-called holy work but the vicar kept asking her, so Mary accepted, then they became good friends.

They often spent their nights debating the scripture of Christ, why God had allowed the war to happen and why God had kept Richard from contacting her. Of course Mary had thrown out the Vicar more than once because he was just talking out of his ass but he was still a good man at heart.

And it wasn't actually like there were many good people left in the village anymore, the vast majority of the evacuees had had to be moved out of the village when the Germans had bombed the school, post office and now the poor lady that used to provide the village with free childcare was dead.

She had died in a massive explosion when the Germans had bombed the school.

Mary still had no idea what she was going to do for a job because there weren't any at all in the village or the neighbouring villages for that matter. She was all alone and Mary had to protect her daughter no matter what.

Because clearly Richard was never coming home for Christmas.

***

25th December 1945

"I'm leaving you Richard," Mary said.

It might have been 7 months since the Germans surrendered in Europe on the 8th May and then Richard had finally come home for Christmas a few days ago but he was a foul man.

Mary had Liebert on her lap as she bounced her precious daughter up and down like she had when the war first started, as her, Liebert and Richard sat around their broken-wooden table that was already missing a wooden leg.

The entire kitchen had been so infected with woodworm now that it was disgusting, foul and Mary hadn't been in the kitchen for ages. She had thankfully gotten enough money from donations in the village to have the woodworm removed but the kitchen couldn't be saved and Mary didn't have enough money to fix it all.

Now Mary cooked, cleaned and washed up in the living room and rarely came out to the kitchen. Sure it was a hard way to live but it was the way that she had been forced by a husband that had never come home to her.

It had been bad enough over the past few years when Mary had had to prostitute herself out to the men in the village to provide food and buy good wood for the fire so she could keep little Liebert warm, but it was even worse when Richard had told her that he had been home for six months.

And he had chosen to only arrive a few days ago.

Five months ago Mary had been skipping meals constantly because she had to provide for Liebert, Mary had been so sick and poorly that she had honestly believed she was going to die, and if Richard had been here then that might not have happened.

And ever since Richard had been home he had been shouting, screaming and even threatening to hit Mary and their daughter because Liebert was crying at the noise. It was clear the war did a number on Richard and she truly respected that.

After the Great War, Mary had spent six months helping returning veterans recover and thankfully so many of them had recovered because they had wanted the help, but Richard didn't. He was only interested in drink, drink and more drink so Mary had sold the house to a lovely young couple and Mary had given Richard some of the money.

He had already spent it on drink because he hadn't been listening to Mary when she had explained she was leaving him last night.

Now it was Christmas morning, Mary had packed up her things and she was leaving her ungrateful, foul drunk of a husband forever. She had only wanted to give him a real Christmas dinner on rations as a thank-you for serving the country and winning the war, but that was the extent to which she felt indebted to him.

There was a loud knock on the front door and Richard started to fall asleep because he was clearly as drunk as ever.

The door opened and the vicar and his wife turned up, Mary and Liebert were going to live with them for a month whilst the paperwork of buying a new flat in London went through because that was taking a while. And at least there were jobs in London, a lot of death and problems but Mary just knew she would be okay.

She had somehow managed to provide for her daughter during a terrible war without a husband so she was more than sure she could survive without one in London not in wartime, and she might have been approaching "old" as the young couple had said to her, but Mary was determined to provide for her daughter no matter what and find a husband again.

And ideally find one that would be home for Christmas.

AVAILABLE AT ALL MAJOR BOOKSELLERS!

FEAST OF DRUNKENNESS
A Contemporary Holiday Fantasy Short Story

31st December 2023
North England, United Kingdom

Witch Aaliyah Jones had never ever liked alcohol, beer or wine. It was just something about the foul taste, the awful smell and the sheer disgusting texture that she didn't like, but right now she was even more disgusted that it seemed like beer was the only thing that could save the entire world from death, destruction and suffering.

Aaliyah stood in a massive golden cavern that stretched for tens of metres up in the air and wide, creating a wonderful and very delightfully spacious cavern for Aaliyah to enjoy. The golden walls of the cavern were smooth and shiny and perfectly warm to the touch that helped to keep the entire cavern not too warm but warm enough so that it was cozy for her to enjoy all year round.

It had been decades since Aaliyah had stepped outside but she always had a massive 80-inch TV playing in the background as she tucked it away with three large red sofas and an oak coffee table in one corner of the cavern.

Right now the TV was playing the local news covering the north of England and it was the normal rubbish. Like the England national football team suffering yet another loss, the government making yet another mistake and there being yet another flood nearby.

Aaliyah was just glad to have the noise playing in the background and the delicious sensational smell of peanut butter cookies baking in the warming black stove oven on the other side of the cavern too. Thankfully it was magically run so it wasn't burning any nasty fossil fuels which made Aaliyah feel better.

She might not have interacted with many humans these past decades but it didn't mean that she didn't want to help them, even if they were the reason why Aaliyah had been hiding in her massive cavern for years.

Aaliyah had always loved the ancient Egyptians and their magic and their mythology. Their magic was so rich and detailed and wonderfully archaic that it was always so pleasurable to dip into those forgotten spells from time to time, well, until she went a little too far.

Back before the second world war when Aaliyah was still in contact with tons of witches and wizards spread out through the entire world and they all tried to help the Allies as best as they could. There was an ancient spell book found by the Nazis in Egypt and so Aaliyah went to retrieve it.

She hadn't realised what the book was until she had killed a good thirty Nazis including the person in control of Egypt for Hitler. But once she had discovered it was a spell book written by the Ancient Gods themselves like Ra, Anubis and Sekhet then she quickly realised it needed to be destroyed.

But she didn't.

Aaliyah stood in the middle of the cavern in front of an ancient cast iron cauldron that was bubbling away as Aaliyah sprinkled in some of the dust from the pages of the book.

It seemed that last night when Aaliyah was reading the book aloud (a very stupid thing to do) she had accidentally reversed time before the Feast of Drunkenness had gotten created in the mythology and the deadly conditions that led to the creation of the December festival.

It seemed that back in ancient Egypt the Sun and Creator God had sent one of his children to destroy humanity because he was bored of their cruelty and nonsense towards each other, but Ra didn't want every single human to die because then no one would be left to learn from the lesson.

Yet the child sent to destroy humanity called Sekhmet couldn't be reasoned with or stopped so Ra had ordered a massive amount of beer to be dyed red because Sekhmet was obsessed with drinking the red blood of humans. So when Sekhmet found the red beer, he drunk it and became reborn as the Lady of Drunkenness Hathor.

And Aaliyah had just erased it from history last night and it was only she was in bed that she had realised she had read aloud a time-warping spell.

Aaliyah had no doubt why the hell the ancient Egyptians wanted such a spell and she had no idea why it had taken her all these decades to read the spell book but she had.

And now she had to fix it.

The TV playing in the background changed to show all the volcanic eruptions, earthquakes and civil wars that had broken out all over the world.

So many people dying in the streets, getting murdered and there were thousands of people drinking the blood of the fallen so readily.

Aaliyah just knew that they were obsessed by Sekhmet so Aaliyah had to fix the problem no matter what.

Thankfully Aaliyah had contacted the Sekhmet through magical means earlier in the day leaking her location so hopefully someone dedicated to the God would turn up sooner or later to kill her but Aaliyah had to be done by then.

"Raise again Old Ones," Aaliyah said over the cauldron hoping that the dust contained in the spell book would help her to reach the ancient Egyptian gods and goddesses that penned the spell book all those thousands of years ago.

Nothing happened.

Aaliyah stomped her foot on the ground. This wasn't what she needed. The Festival of Drunkenness had always happened in December and that was where the most magical power would be held so Sekhmet had to be stopped today before it became January and the magic held in December was lost.

Aaliyah danced her fingers over the bubbling liquid and it all became blood red instantly and Aaliyah had decided to try something a little stronger than normal beer. The ancient Egyptians had only ever tried beer because it was all they had.

But the world had come a long way since then so Aaliyah was cooking up a lot of magically enhanced vodka to hopefully get Sekhmet even more sleepy.

The entire cavern shook violently.

The TV fell to the ground. Shattering.

Cracks appeared in the golden walls.

Immense chunks of rock collapsed around her.

Aaliyah cursed under her breath. It was too soon. The alcohol wasn't ready yet and it was still needed another ten minutes.

A puff of black smoke appeared in front of Aaliyah on the opposite side of the cauldron.

It was a figure made up of pure shadow and clearly the figure didn't want to reveal its true form but Aaliyah recognised the cold, icy presence and her increasing urge to kill something.

Aaliyah forced herself to focus and not absorb the sheer aura of murder, chaos and blood drinking that was coming from the figure.

Sekhmet was here.

Sekhmet orgasmed a little as Aaliyah felt more magical energy pour into the cavern and she just knew that it was the magic from drinking the blood of innocent murdered people.

"This is not right," Aaliyah said hoping to buy herself some time.

"The end of the world is far more than Ra ever deemed good," Sekhmet said. "Ra was a fool and you were the greater fool for erasing what happened to me. Now tell me, is that beer, gin or wine?"

Aaliyah remained silent.

"It would make sense for a human to try and recreate the event that created the Festival of Drunkenness and me turning into Hathor," Sekhmet said. "But I know what happened and now humanity will burn for *your* mistakes,"

Aaliyah looked down at the blood red liquid and it looked so magical and inviting. She so badly wanted to lick it and feed her sexy god that would reward her for her service.

No.

Aaliyah just looked at Sekhmet. He was a foul creature that had to die for what he was doing to the world.

Aaliyah shot out her hand.

Sekhmet flicked his shadowy fingers and Aaliyah felt extremely cold.

She had lost her magic.

Aaliyah didn't know how Sekhmet had managed to do that but she felt so cold, alone and isolated, like a massive part of herself was dead and was never returning to her.

"You cannot hurt me human," Sekhmet said. "And now you have lost all the strength that your magic gave you to resist me,"

Aaliyah shrugged because she actually felt no different in that department. She knew that Sekhmet had feasted on her magic so it was gone but she was a human that meant she had some sort of power left.

She just didn't know what that power was.

Sekhmet pointed a single shadowy finger at Aaliyah and her ears were filled with the screaming of people in the streets, the roaring flames of fires and the screaming bullets of guns.

"I admit," Sekhmet said, "I like humanity more these days. You are more divided, stupid and have much better weapons to slaughter others with then you did in my day,"

Aaliyah hated herself for allowing this to happen but maybe that was the solution to all of this.

If the spell book had created the problem in the first place then it also had to be the solution. Sekhmet had just said it himself that humanity these days were more stupid than the ancient Egyptians so the Egyptians had to be smart enough to know how to reverse this.

"Isis," Aaliyah said staring into the beautifully blood red liquid, "I know you wrote a section of the spell book. Return to the land of the living Goddess of Magic,"

"Ha," Sekhmet said. "You think you can simply utter non-powerful words and expect to defeat me,"

Aaliyah kept looking at the red liquid but nothing happened and she felt Sekhmet stand right next to her.

He grabbed her hand.

Pushing her hand into the cauldron.

Aaliyah screamed underwater. Searing heat engulfed her flesh.

Aaliyah cried down in agony. Tears streamed off her face. Then nothing.

Aaliyah didn't feel the cold fingers of Sekhmet pushing her head into the cauldron but she couldn't move so he was still holding her.

She didn't feel any of the boiling, searing or agonising heat engulfing her skin, Aaliyah only felt coldness.

"I cannot return to you," Isis said. "I cannot help you more than what you have all already done but your original plan is the way to win magic or no magic,"

Aaliyah instantly understood what she needed to do.

Aaliyah stomped her feet on Sekhmet's feet.

He screamed and released her.

Aaliyah elbowed him in the ribs.

Sekhmet fell backwards.

Aaliyah grabbed his head.

Pushing him into the cauldron.

Aaliyah held him in with all the strength she had.

Sekhmet laughed under the red liquid.

Then he laughed as he drank all the liquid and within moments the Caudron was empty and Aaliyah felt his body go very limb, drunk and she watched as the shadowiness of his body fade away.

Revealing nothing in its place.

Aaliyah felt a tat of her magic return to her and she instantly clicked her fingers and the TV repaired itself and returned to the news. And it really did show that nothing was wrong with the world.

In fact, there were no bad news stories whatsoever. There wasn't a single murder, natural disaster or anything happening in the world today and it was funny to see the news producer struggling to find anything interesting to show their viewers.

Because Aaliyah instantly knew that she had managed to fix history, recreate Hathor and she had managed to resurrect all the dead people that had been killed when Sekhmet attacked the world once more, and now everything was right with the world.

Of course it was just for a single day but that was enough. For a single New Year's Eve, the entire world could be happy, content and joyous for a few more precious hours and that was perfectly okay with Aaliyah.

She had to heal herself first and get changed and do herself some makeup but then she was going to go out in the world and witness what exactly she had saved today.

Because for the first time in decades she was going to be a real person and that excited her a lot more than she ever wanted to admit.

AVAILABLE AT ALL MAJOR BOOKSELLERS!

POISONING THE WINTER VILLAGE CONTEST
A Holiday Mystery Short Story

19th December 2022
Southeast England

Now I fully believe that the vast majority of small villages, towns and even cities have some sort of flat out weird contest for the holiday season. I once lived in a village that had a "Best Peppermint Cream" contest and that was a particularly great year because I do love all things peppermint, but there are some holiday traditions. Including "The Best Killer Santa Costume" that was probably the weirdest I've come across but I'm sure there are plenty more out there.

And you see before I continue any further I actually need you to understand weird this village is that I live in, and just how crazy how of the traditions are so you can understand that what I ended up doing was relatively sane compared to the contests.

You see my name is Jo-Jo O'Dell and I seriously love the holidays, Christmas trees and anything to do with peppermint. And up until three days ago I worked as the Chief Operations Manager for the county's sanitation network.

I loved my job because I was so good at it. I completely updated their prehistoric computer systems, I made the sanitation network more effective and cheaper to run and I was beloved by everyone.

Well, that's what I thought.

But it turns out in very conservative rural Southeast England, people don't like it when a gay man comes into the village with his husband, Patrick, over twenty years and two beautiful children, gets the top job at the only real employment centre in the area and manages to outdo everyone.

So apparently, there was a complaint made against me, because *apparently* I was being a bad worker, my bosses refused to support me and well, I got the sack for nothing that I did and the initial complaints were all lies anyway.

Tonight I would thankfully get my revenge though.

I was standing with my amazing hunk of a husband who was easily a foot taller than me with massive muscles, an insanely hot body and a slight blond beard that I have to admit I did like playing with at night.

Our two wonderful children were having a sleepover with their best friends tonight, and they were 17-year-olds anyway, so we were standing in the massive town hall structure that was very impressive for a small town/ village. I really liked its large white marble pillars with gold veining that helped to add such depth and texture to the large square hall.

The walls were freshly painted cream, the ceiling was a little patching but poor Jim had to do the painting and he was unfortunately half-blind so I'm amazed he managed this much. I just wished he took the money I offered him to go and get the surgery to fix his sight.

He refused and spat at my feet.

The entire hall was covered in beautiful Christmas decorations with massive banters, streams of tinsel and child-made paper chains in a rainbow of colours hung from everywhere. And the sweet aromas of wonderful peppermint, ginger and mulled wine filled the air making the sensational taste of Christmas cake form on my tongue.

"Evening Jo-Jo," an elderly woman said as she walked past me.

I smiled at her because Mrs Oliver was a great woman, she was kind, helpful and seriously hadn't cared when she caught me and Patrick making out in the closet of the town hall. And amazingly enough that actually kicked off a friendship with the elderly lady for twenty years.

Amazing how things worked out.

"Is everything set up for tonight?" Patrick asked me with a devilish grin.

I simply nodded because it was only two hours ago that Patrick had told me he had also been fired from working in the local council because of lies, deceit and corruption so I told him my plan and he wanted to help.

Of course by this point there was nothing to help with but I told him to enjoy the sight.

Because the thing about two gay men that met each other when we were both homeless, hungry and very angry at our parents for kicking us out because we were gay, was that we were rather cruel to people that we didn't like. Just like how the world was cruel to us for no reason whatsoever.

As soon as I was fired I used my sanitation knowledge and put it to good use because the interesting thing about sanitation networks is they are very, very prone to breaking. Especially when a certain person, also known as me, knows exactly what values to shut off and my bosses at the local council never ever thought to actually lock me out of the system.

Well, even if they had it wouldn't have saved them because I had used over twenty different backdoors for myself so I could get into the computer system whenever I wanted. And wow, have I been busy over the past few days and now everything was going to show up.

And things were going to get very interesting, very quickly because the water tank in the town hall that supplied the building with drinking water was currently being flooded with wee-water.

"Places everyone!" a young and rather hot man shouted.

I had never really liked the Deputy Major too much because he wasn't exactly friendly towards my kids, my house and Mrs Oliver so I was looking forward to teaching him a lesson on tonight of all nights.

Because tonight was The Village Winter Contest which involved two things, both were things that I highly approved of and normally entered myself. The first part of the contest was who could make the best peppermint drink in the entire village and the second part was who could make the best miniature village.

All around us there were massive wooden tables with young and older, fat and slim and hip and seriously not people standing behind them with large mugs on the tables.

It was so amazing to smell all the different cocktails, mocktails and soft drinks get mixed together to create the best peppermint drink ever. The hall was filled with delightful sounds of banging, stirring and panicked voices scared about getting something wrong.

It was all rubbish of course because the so-called prize money a person was meant to get never arrived in their bank account. There were plenty of theories over the years why but I knew that it went into the Mayor's bank account and no one seemed to care.

Almost no one.

That was one of the advantages of having a husband that worked with computers, had a Masters degree in computer science and basically had no problem breaking laws to help people. I really did love that man so we *might* have hacked the Mayor's bank account and now all the winners from the past twenty years had their prize money, with interest of course.

"What about the water?" my beautiful husband asked me.

I laughed. "Just relax babe,"

Now he did have a good point in all fairness because I was now quickly realising that barely anyone here tonight was using water in their special drinks. Which I supposed was because I might have also added a little, chemical substance that would give whoever drank the water horrific diaherria.

And before you think about it, no this couldn't hurt anyone because I had already set off an alarm and prescheduled a warning message to be sent out at a certain time. Meaning the problem should be detected after the judges drink the water but before anyone else does.

I'm sure some of you might be wondering

what I have against the four judges tonight, but let me tell you I have every single damn right to poison these people. The first and dickhead judge was the Mayor himself, the second was the Deputy Mayor and the third was the local history teacher.

Now I actively encourage people to learn outside the things that school teaches you because school is rather limited in the grand scheme of things and I understand why. There's only so much you can learn in the school day.

But when the local teacher, a local woman called Elizabeth, decided to cover LGBT+ History, I was interested because I didn't know that much myself. But to point to my kids in the middle of the history lesson and talk *about* them like they weren't in the room, they weren't real people and they were mere examples of equalities, that was pushing her luck I thought.

It was even worse when she concluded her mini-lecture by commenting on how *the kids turned out well considering the sheer lack of femineity and masculinity in their lives.* Well even now I have no idea what I would say to her but at least my daughter and son had some… choice words for the teacher.

I do love my family.

And the fourth final judge bless him, was a Old Doc George, the local doctor who was really trying to force me and my husband to be sterilized so we didn't spread our gay DNA to anyone else.

Need I say more?

"Can the first contestant come up?" the old fat mayor said as he sat down at the wooden table on the far end of the town hall.

My beautiful husband grinned on as a little middle-aged man bought up a tray containing four large glasses of piping hot peppermint hot chocolate and this man certainly would have used water from the town hall.

All four judges gulped down the drink, had a massive overdramatic gasp and quietly wrote notes about the drink in their little black notebooks.

"Next," the Mayor said.

I was a little confused as to why my wee-water plan wasn't working immediately but I was a patient man.

Next a very tall elegant lady wearing a long sweeping white dress walked past us holding a very large trap filled with a peppermint malt drink. Again she would have used the water from the town hall.

The judges smiled, gulped down their drink and gasped again. They laughed at each other because they had a malt moustache under their noses and they made their silly little notes.

"I thought-"

I kissed my husband on the lips to shut him up because I really couldn't understand why the plan wasn't working.

"Third one," the mayor said but I noticed something was wrong with his voice. It sounded strained.

A very young teenage girl went over to the judges with three shot glasses filled with her clean liquid.

The whole cycle continued again but after the judges wrote down the notes in their notebooks they started frowning at each other.

They all farted again and again until they didn't.

Then things got very, very messy for everyone. And things got very, very funny for the two of us.

***

I think the most amazing thing about poisoning people without anyone knowing that you've actually done it is very simple. It is that when shit hits the fan rather literally and all the sanitation warning systems go off, everyone turns to you, you get your old job back with tenure and double the salary in exchange for "helping" them get rid of the problem.

So after the chocolate fountains started and everyone got the emergency warning about the sanitation system failing all over the county, the mayor rushed over to me and begged me to help him.

I did in exchange for the double the pay and tenure position, so now I really couldn't get sacked now forever.

In all fairness it had only taken me two hours to fix my problem but a good hour of that was me just deleting any evidence that I had contaminated the system, and for good measure I played on my phone for another two hours so I made it look like it was an impossible job that only I could do.

And it worked and all without a single innocent person getting ill too. That was perfect.

No one saw the judges for the next two weeks, no one won this year's Village Winter Contest but at least the prize money somehow ended up in all the contestant's bank accounts, even the ones I didn't like, and even some charities benefited.

That husband of mine, if it was actually him of course, was a great man that I seriously loved more than anything in the world.

And with my revenge done, my job returned to me and now I had twice as much money, I really was looking forward to Christmas because it seriously was a magical time of year where literally anything could happen.

Now if you don't mind as I mentioned earlier, my two children are staying at their friend's for the night so me and my husband have some alone time.

And believe me, we definitely plan to make good, wholesome use of it.

AVAILABLE AT ALL MAJOR BOOKSELLERS!

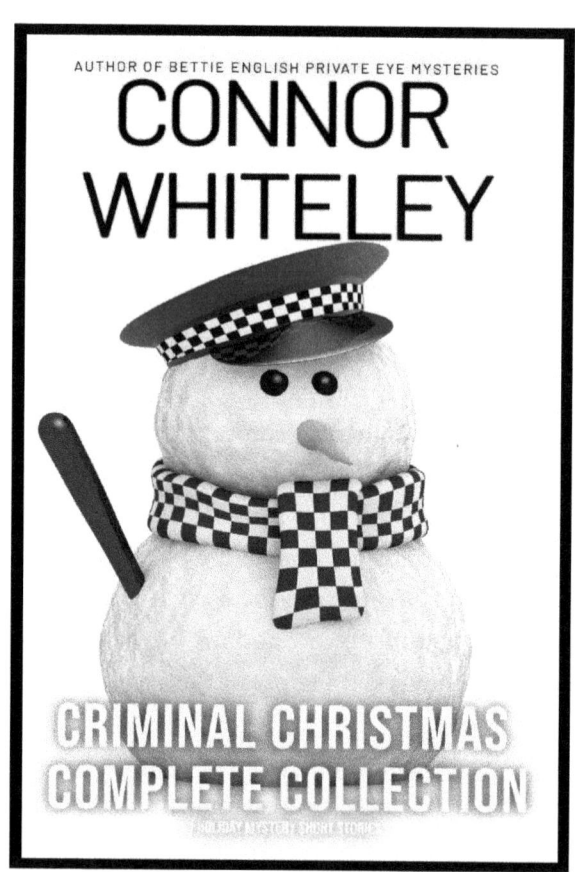

BESTSELLING AUTHOR OF WAY OF THE ODYSSEY
CONNOR WHITELEY

MURDER
A LADY TANO FANTASY ADVENTURE NOVELLA

MURDER
A Lady Tano Fantasy Adventure Novella

CHAPTER 1

I had to stop a mass murderer no matter the cost.

I, Lady Ithane Tano, pulled the large black hood of my cloak as tight as I could over my head as I went inside the Joyous Tavern. It was a rather interesting, if not a little tasteless establishment in a town in the middle of nowhere.

I actually rather liked how cold it was with a dying fire in the middle of the large tavern, and its brown sticky walls, ceiling and floor were hardly any better. It was like all the light in the tavern had come here to die because it was so dark I could barely make out where I was going let alone the people in here.

I made my part towards the "barely" lit bar, that was nothing more than a slab of rotting wood next to the firepit. There was a tall elderly man standing behind there and he had clocked me as soon as I had come in.

In fact, everyone had.

In the tiny amounts of light given off by the dying candles loosely attached to iron fixtures on the walls, I managed to make out dirty faces that were frowning, judging and looking at me like I was a piece of meat.

I was never going to provoke these people because they were just minding their own business. They were sitting around their small (?) wooden tables nursing drinks and quietly talking about their lives.

There was no reason for them to be threats to me and I wasn't going to talk to them, because I was here for a different purpose. I was here for information about a man that had come through this town a few days ago. I was here hunting the man that had killed millions of my people, had made me lose my empire and who had killed me before the Goddess had resurrected me.

I was hunting Maric and he was going to die so he could never ever hurt another person again.

As soon as I got to the bar, the elderly man clicked his fingers and all the candles in the tavern got brighter. I smiled because that was a nice trick and now I could see everyone a little too well for my liking.

I'm sure my powers and magic from the Goddess would have allowed me to see all the knives, swords and crossbows on the tables but I was new to this. I didn't know how my new powers worked yet.

The awful aroma of burning fat from the candles made me cough a little and the tavern was filling with the hissing of burning, dripping fat and the mutterings of the patrons.

"There was a man that came to this town three days ago," I said to the elderly man. "He would have been an outsider, a tall and well-educated man, maybe even extremely arrogant. Do you know him?"

I heard three people get up and I moved my hands down to the hilts of my two longswords. I didn't even try to hide the action because I wanted them to know I was serious.

I was serving the Goddess and trying to protect the innocent here, so no one was stopping me finding Maric.

The elderly man grinned. "Yeah I know him he came through three days ago like ya said. Him and his men stayed the night and he paid me a thousand Gold to watch over you in case you came here,"

I shook my head as I heard every single man in the tavern stand up and they grabbed their weapons.

"I don't want to kill you," I said meaning every word of it. "But in the name of the Goddess I will give you one chance to walk away. Do that and I will not come after you,"

The elderly man grabbed a sword from under the bar.

"Kill her!" he shouted.

I spun around and felt the wonderful and delightful golden divine energy of the Goddess fill me.

My bright golden armour glowed even brighter. Shadowy golden wings grew out of my back and my eyes burnt with the divine fury of the Goddess.

"Heretics!" I shouted.

The men flew at me.

They swung their swords.

They fired their crossbows.

They threw their knives.

I flew at them.

I became a blur to them.

I swung my sword.

Chomping into flesh.

Blood sprayed up walls.

I clicked my fingers.

The bolts melted.

As did the knives.

The men ran for the doors.

I couldn't allow them to escape and hurt more innocent people.

I shot out my hands.

A fireball shot out.

Engulfing men in flames.

They screamed.

I flew forward.

Slashing. Lashing. Killing as I went.

Within a few moments all the foul heretics were dead and all my divine power drained away as there were no more guilty abusers or evil people to kill, my mission was done for just a moment. Which really was a wonderful feeling.

"You witch," the elderly man said.

I turned around and went over to him as the elderly man coughed as his lungs stopped working.

The foul aroma of charred flesh, fat candles and burning wood as the tavern was starting to go up in flames filled the air.

"Where is Maric?" I asked the elderly man.

He laughed. "You cannot find him because you are stupid and you are thick and you are nothing,"

I tapped into the power of the Goddess and I charged my voice with as much magical power as I could.

"Tell me what I want to know," I said my voice booming. "Where is Maric?"

The elderly man laughed. "Your magic has no power stupid woman,"

The man started coughing again and I could sense how much pain and agony he was in, so as much as he didn't deserve it, I punched him in the face. Killing him instantly so he was no longer in pain.

I stood up, went behind the bar to grab the thousand Gold so I could donate it to a local charity and then I simply allowed the entire tavern to go up in flames.

I was still no closer to finding Maric and that annoyed me a lot more than I ever wanted to admit.

CHAPTER 2

Witchfinder Alexender Quill flat out hated the foul, awfully twisted forest that him and his best friend Maxine were walking through. He just hated how the massive oak, pine and chestnut trees were growing at strange angles that just shouldn't be possible.

The trees were so bent and twisted and had roots growing out of the top that Alexander just wasn't sure if he wanted to be here or not. But he kept on walking because he had a job to do for the beautiful, sexy Lady Ithane Tano.

And he was never going to fail her.

Alexander rather liked the sweet aromas of vanilla, Camille and roasted chestnuts that filled the air. He didn't doubt the great aromas were just a part of the forest's cheap tricks with its creepy white mist that surrounded him, but he didn't mind the smell.

He stepped over thick branches that rose up from the black ground like claws as he kept going and he would have preferred to see some green leaves when he looked up. Instead he only saw black twisted roots where branches were meant to be and dim lights fighting to get through black clouds.

None of this was natural and Alexender placed a firm hand on the hilt of his sword and his other hand on the hilt of his Blessed Dagger.

"Where's this witch meant to be?" Maxine asked.

Alexander smiled as he stepped over yet another branch. He had only been with Maxine and beautiful Ithane for two months now, and he was loving every minute of it. Maxine might have been a young woman who lived and breathed the city life when he had met her, but she was amazing and taking to outdoor life really well.

She was slightly ahead of him but Alexander was impressed her long brown hair was flowing around like it had a mind of its own without getting caught on any branches or anything. Alexander had already had to cut off some of his longish brown hair after a branch decided to attack him.

"The witch is meant to be up ahead," Alexander said.

He still wasn't sure why Ithane had wanted him of all people to come into the forest and track down the witch. He was a Witchfinder so that meant he liked hunting down rogue witches, wizards and warlocks to see if they were a threat.

But he hated bothering good magic users that were just minding their own business.

"Wow," Maxine said as she stopped.

Alexender went over to her and he shivered as he walked into a wall of heat so he took another step forward. And he was amazed that he had walked into a large clearing covered in thick green grass and golden sunshine in the middle of the forest.

There was a large mushroom house in the middle of the clearing and an elven woman leaning against the mushroom.

Small voices came from behind Alexander and he smiled as about a hundred or maybe even a thousand tiny mushroom people with tiny little sticks came up behind them.

One mushroom person came up to Alexender and thrusted the stick into his ankle.

Alexander leapt forward and hissed in pain.

"Naughty Donald," the elven woman said. "I am so sorry, they are normally a lot better behaved than that,"

Alexender had no idea what to make of the woman but she seemed friendly enough and she didn't want to hurt them, for now.

"It's okay," Alexander said stepping forward with Maxine close behind him. "Me and my friend wanted to ask for your help please in exchange for some herbs we found on the way here,"

Alexender gestured Maxine to get out the large piles of herbs and flowers they had picked on the way here.

The elven woman came over and Alexender noticed the mushroom people were getting a little touchy.

The woman smiled as she inspected the herbs and flowers.

"These are really fresh and quite lovely. I will help you with whatever you desire within reason," the woman said taking the piles and tossing them to the mushroom people.

Alexender was impressed the mushroom

people caught the piles perfectly and carried them away like they were feathers. And not ten times heavier than the mushrooms themselves.

"I love them," Maxine said.

Alexander laughed. He was really impressed how well Maxine was taking all of this.

"Lady Ithane Tano would like your help finding Maric please," Alexander said.

The elven woman laughed. "Everyone knows she's alive by the way and I am glad about that. She is an amazing woman, she gave millions a chance for a better life and I hope she rules again,"

Alexander completely agreed. Ithane had to be the most incredible woman he had ever met too, but he didn't say that.

"Maric is currently in the City of Barbara and Lady Barabara is hosting him on behalf of Azrael,"

Alexander and Maxine both hissed at the mention of Azrael. Alexander flat out hated that evil twisted man that was pulling strings all over the world, killing heads of state and organising the destruction of Ithane's empire.

Azrael was a monster and Alexander wanted to find him and end him so he could never hurt another innocent person again.

"But I will warn you Witchfinder," the woman said. "You come from the village of Monotoney on the other side of the world. Your village has attracted the glaze of Azrael for a reason I cannot see and your family, friends and everyone who protected you is in danger,"

Alexander took a few steps back and almost stepped on a mushroom person. He couldn't believe she knew where he was from, and he couldn't go back there. He couldn't protect everyone from Azrael and whoever was working on his behalf.

He just couldn't.

The woman smiled as she went back over to her mushroom house. "You must make a decision in two days times about your actions. If you leave on the third morning there is a good chance you can save your people from Azrael's annihilation. If not you decide not to intervene then your village will be annihilated,"

Alexander wanted to protest and shout and scream at her because she had to be wrong. He could not go back to that place, he just couldn't. And yet this woman was telling him he had to, who did she think she was?

Then she went back inside the mushroom house and Alexander blinked and he found himself and Maxine just standing there on the side of a dirt road.

"What do you want to do?" Maxine asked. "I can find Ithane and deal with Maric if you want to leave now,"

Alexander shook his head. He had two days to make a decision and maybe that would be enough time to deal with Maric so all of them could go.

"Let's just find Ithane. Let's deal with Maric and make sure he can never hurt another innocent person again,"

Alexander didn't even give Maxine time to reply as he stormed off down the road to find the beautiful woman he loved.

And maybe she would know what to do about this nightmare choice.

CHAPTER 3

I flat out couldn't believe how my powers were still temperamental and they didn't work when I needed them to. It was so annoying that I couldn't influence that elderly man to tell me what had happened to Maric, it would have been a disaster if sexy Alexender hadn't had better luck.

I gently rode with Alexender and Maxine on their own black and brown horses either side of me, on a wide dirt road. It was wonderfully wide and I really did like the warm breeze that brushed my cheeks.

It was nice to be somewhere that smelt clean with hints of pine, damp and mint filling the air. It was so much better than the smell of that awful tavern, and it was great that I had met a convoy of carriages a few miles back working for a local charity providing free healthcare for the poorest in the world.

They were very happy with the extra thousand Gold.

I kept flicking my gaze to the immense oak, pine and chestnut trees that lined the road. They were all naturally straight with their large branches stretching out away from the road, which was a lot better than what sexy Alexender had told me about his own adventure in the forest.

"What do you know about Lady Barabara?" Maxine asked.

I smiled because it was all I could do as the wonderfully warm sunlight beamed down on me. It was such a nice day and I was doing everything in my power not to think about Lady Barabara and what the hell she had done to maintain that little pathetic title of hers.

You see I was a Lady because my father had died so I ruled over the Tanoian Empire. I outlawed discrimination, improved living standards and my empire was the only place in the world that had reached true equality.

And everyone loved me.

Whereas Lady Barabara had slept her way to the top of another empire, the Plotmeny Empire, and she had wanted to be called a Lady for the sake of being a pretend Noblewoman.

She was not noble at all. Especially after she killed her two sisters, her parents and her little brother once he reached 18.

"Not a lot really," I said knowing it was a minor lie. "She's a user and not a real noblewoman but I haven't seen her in years,"

"When did you last see her?" Alexender asked.

I really did love the wonderful sound of his voice. It was so smooth, manly and it was just great to listen to.

"Maybe five years ago just after my Ascension to Lady," I said. "Lady Barabara had invited me to her City to make me an offer about killing Plotmeny on her behalf,"

"I thought Emperor Plotmeny and her were married?" Maxine asked.

I laughed and moved my horse to one side to avoid a massive pothole.

"You really have been in the City too long," Alexender said to her. "When it comes to power, men and women are just as bad about plotting their access to influence. Sometimes I've been on jobs and it isn't the magic users you need to watch out for. It's the people in power,"

"Exactly," I said as I noticed something strange up ahead.

I frowned as I noticed three white horses with flags on their backs. Their riders were wearing the bright white armour of the

Plotmeny Empire and the flags showed the same.

"Let me to the talking. Otherwise we are all dead," I said.

I didn't like running into border patrols this early on because they were always touchy, interfering and evil but I wasn't going to hurt them. They were just innocent people doing their jobs and that was never a reason to hurt people.

"Stop in the name of the Emperor," one of the men said.

I gently brought my horse to a stop and I was pleased that Maxine was starting to get better on horses. She wouldn't have been able to do that so artfully last week.

"What is your business in this area? And where are your permits?" a man asked but I couldn't tell which one.

"I am on diplomatic business for the state of the Tanoian Empire," I said with as much authority as I could.

I knew there was a chance they knew my empire had been destroyed two months ago, but some news travelled slower than others.

"The Tanoian Empire was destroyed months ago and we are grateful that it was," the men said.

I frowned and pretended like I hadn't experienced the burning of my cities, the burning of my people and the streets running with blood.

"What?" I asked pretending as much as I could. "Are you sure? I left three months ago for diplomatic work,"

One of the men came over to me and placed a gentle hand on my shoulder.

"I am so sorry for your loss," the man said. "It isn't easy losing your country but I have to ask what business brought you here?"

I pretended to cry a little. "I was meant to visit Lady Barabara for trade talks,"

The men looked at each other.

The man took his hand off my shoulder. "Lady Barabara already has guests I am afraid and not good ones either. You can deal with her as much as you want but be very careful,"

I pretended to cry a little more but I could sense that he was hiding something. And all the men looked very concerned for our welfare and I knew that Lady Barabara had pissed off her husband for the last time.

I wasn't sure what was happening but Emperor Plotmeny was making a move against his wife.

And I just didn't want to get caught in the crossfire of a political war.

Not for a single second.

CHAPTER 4

Alexender was seriously impressed with how brilliantly Ithane had handled those guards. She might have been one of the most capable people he had ever met, but he had dealt with Plotmeny guards before and they were hardline idiots that didn't care about killing.

It only made him like her even more.

Alexander rode with Ithane and Maxine behind him towards the immense black iron gates of the City of Barabara. Alexander was surprised how massive and strange the city looked compared to the glorious spires of the Tanoian empire.

Alexander was probably a mile away from the gates and he hated how he could only see a massive black stone castle in the middle of the city. He couldn't see any docks, any spires of towers for the innocent people to live and work in, nor defend.

In fact Alexender couldn't see any defenses at all. Not on the black city walls, not on the gates, not even in the massive wheat fields that surrounded the city.

Alexender shook his head as Maxine came up next to him. He really liked how she was wide-eyed, taking everything in like this was the most impressive sight of her life.

Maybe it was. Alexender knew she wasn't a native to the Tanoian empire but she had spent most of her life there so she was used to living like a queen despite her only being a poor person (well that's what she would be if she lived in a normal empire).

"This isn't right," Ithane said.

Alexender looked at her. "What do you mean? This looks like every other city in this part of the world because the rich get their castle and the poor people probably have shacks,"

Ithane stopped and Alexender didn't dare go on without her. He didn't doubt there were guards watching them from the gates so he knew Ithane wouldn't be doing something that looked odd without good reason.

"I sense something wrong here. The Goddess is telling me something about corruption, guilt and abuse here,"

Alexender forced himself not to roll his eyes. He was more than grateful for this Goddess bringing back the woman he was falling for but this was the state of the world.

"And something darker is going on in that City," Ithane said as she started her horse moving again.

Alexender looked at Maxine and she didn't look sure. He hoped Ithane was wrong but as much as he just wanted to focus on finding and killing Maric (and forgetting about his home village under threat), he just knew he was going to have to do something about the corruption in this city.

He had to protect the innocent in any way he could.

Alexender kept leading them towards the black gates and he smiled when they roared open and ten bright white guards on horses rode out to meet them.

They were coming out quickly and he made the others move their horses to one side. Alexender was surprised they didn't stop and they were moving so fast it blew his hair.

"I wonder what's happening," Alexender said.

"Whatever it is," Ithane said riding forwards, "I think we're all walking into something far, far bigger than Maric,"

"Agreed," Maxine said.

Alexender rode towards the black gates and he just went through the still-open gates. It was beyond strange that there were no guards, no soldiers and no one to question why they had entered the city.

Alexender stopped his horse and jumped off. He landed in some awfully stinky wet mud that rose up to his ankles (at least he hoped it was only mud) and he couldn't see anyone.

There were only massive black wooden shacks with little planks running between the other shacks so no one had to walk in the mud. They all looked like they were about to collapse at any moment and some of the roofs already had holes in.

The houses creeped, cracked and the wind howled around them but Alexender wanted, needed to hear some voices. He wanted to know if there were other people in the city but there wasn't.

He was completely alone with Ithane and Maxine and that concerned him a lot more than he ever wanted to admit.

Even to the woman he was falling for.

CHAPTER 5

I whipped out my two swords as I stepped into that awfully stinky mud that was must certainly poo in places. I just couldn't believe what the hell had happened to the City of Barabara. I hated seeing the innocent people having to live in these wooden shacks.

I had learnt a lot about disease, infections and why poor housing had to be destroyed from my Governess as a child. It was outrageous that these shacks still stood where disease, trench foot and so much illness could be created.

It was why I had fought and put so much money into the housing of my subjects so no one would have to die from diseases that didn't need to develop in the first place. Clearly Barabara didn't care about her subjects.

This was an outrage.

But the more I focused on the black shacks, the sheer silence of the city besides the gently howling wind and the thick mud that covered the ground, the more I realised there were no people here.

"Show me Goddess what you see," I said.

I smiled as the wonderful warmth of my Goddess filled my body, mind and soul and I saw exactly what she saw here.

My senses were immediately overwhelmed by the sheer aroma of death, rot and decay. It smelt like a thousand, no a million corpses were rotting in the city on a hot summer's day. I wanted to choke, scream and gag but I didn't.

I was fairly sure the smell was symbolic at best because there must have been a lot of murders and death here. Or maybe there were a lot of murders to come unless I could stop whatever was meant to happen.

Everything in the city had a tint of blood red to it like the entire city had blood on its hands and I could hear something in the distance.

It sounded like two nobles talking, laughing and chanting something strange and demonic in a language I didn't understand. Or better yet the Goddess didn't understand and that just scared me.

I turned around to see what the Goddess thought of the surrounding areas and I could see millions of tiny mushroom people standing there. I had no idea what they meant but maybe they were meant to be a cute way of the Goddess telling me soldiers or whatever would be here at some point.

"Thank you Goddess," I said.

I felt her warmth pulse through me a final time before my vision turned to normal and I bit my lip. Alexender looked stunning with his fit body, sexy longish brown hair and wonderfully broad shoulders.

I was glad he was here with me.

"What did you see?" he asked.

"I'm not entirely sure but I think unless we find out what happened here quickly then I doubt these people are going to stay alive for much longer,"

"Like my home village," Alexender said balling his hands into fists.

I wanted to hug him or something but we had a mission to do and I wasn't sure what I could do to help him. I didn't know much about his past as a teenager but it clearly wasn't happy, and I suppose it was only hard knowing that Azrael was behind the threat.

I would have to talk to him later but I had to focus on the City right now.

I started walking through the thick smelly mud and I gagged every few steps.

I smiled as Maxine went to jump up onto the wooden planks between the shacks but it broke straight away.

And Maxine landed in a massive pile of poo and mud. She gagged but to her credit she stood up like it was exactly what she had meant to do.

She started walking over to me. "No, no, no," I said. "You are not walking next to me smelling like that,"

She poked her tongue out at me. And I clicked my fingers and some of the poo burnt away from her.

"Thanks," she said, "but what's the plan when we make it to the castle?"

"I'm more concerned about the people for now," I said, "but there has to be an explanation. When I was last here there were thousands of people. They might not have been happy or thriving but they were cheerful,"

"And how do you get rid of thousands of people?" Alexender asked just before gagging on the smell.

"I don't know and I'm pretty sure the Goddess doesn't know either," I said, "but still, something is going on here. Why did the Guards leave the city before we arrived? What is Plotmeny going to do to his wife? What did the patrol want to warn us about but didn't?"

"I don't know," Maxine said, looking greener by the second.

I could only nod because there were so many questions and so little time to find out because something was happening in this city and I had no idea what it was.

No idea at all.

CHAPTER 6

Alexender was so relieved as he followed Ithane and Maxine into the massive throne room of the castle that he didn't have to put up with that awful smelly mud anymore. He didn't might the throne room with its jet black stone walls, high domed ceiling and suits of black armour lining the walls. The only way he could tell the armour apart from the wall was because of the odd golden highlights that highlighted the edges.

Alexander enjoyed the sweet aromas of cinnamon, nutmeg and vanilla that filled the throne room, because it left the great taste of spiced tarts like his mother used to make back in his home village on his tongue.

He shook the great memory away, because his home village was the very, very end thing he wanted to think about. He had a mission to do and he had to protect Ithane no matter the cost. There wasn't any room for silly memories about a place he just couldn't go back to.

Alexender was surprised how every sound echoed around the throne room. Every footstep, every breath, every movement. All of it was amplified and echoed off the smooth black walls, and Alexender was glad they would know if anyone was coming behind them.

"Look at the thrones," Maxine said.

Alexender looked at where she was standing and he went over there with Ithane. The two immense silver and bronze thrones were smashed, sliced and murdered beyond all recognition. He wasn't actually sure if these were thrones or dining room chairs.

He knelt down on the ground and moved some of the metal fragments.

Images of death, murder and pain filled his mind. Alexender hissed in pain. His hands burnt with magical energy and a headache corkscrewed across his forehead.

"Ouch," Maxine said trying to tap into his mind. "What the hell did you do?"

Alexender let go of the metal shards. "My magic sometimes picks up memories or emotional traces from objects. Whatever happened here it was bloody and violent,"

Ithane shook her head. "And yet we cannot see the blood or damage with our human eyes,"

Alexender smiled. He knew that Ithane wasn't calling him a liar but she made a good point. There were no marks, dents or signs of an attack in the throne room besides the two thrones.

He had done his fair share of attacking and kidnapping rogue magic users, but he had never bothered being this clean and tidy. Something was wrong and weird about this situation.

"What if this entire situation isn't meant for us?" Ithane asked finding the situation wrong and weird. "What if this scene was set for followers of Azrael that would investigate the disappearance of Maric?"

Alexender nodded. He supposed it could be true but if that was the case then how would Emperor Plotmeny know people would come looking for Maric?

"What about these suits?" Alexender asked.

He whipped out his sword and dagger and Ithane's eyes glowed bright gold. Maybe she was tapping into the Goddess's power but Alexender just knew something wasn't right here.

"Three armed men and a witch stormed the castle," Ithane said. "Maric and Lady Barabara were sitting on the thrones laughing and making fun of the Emperor,"

Alexender shook his head. Lady Barabara was way too ambitious for his liking and she was clearly willing to make a dark bargain just to gain even more power.

"The men came in and killed the guards and they pushed the suits of armour against the wall," Ithane said. "The witch captured Barabara and Maric but she did not work for the Emperor,"

Alexender rolled his eyes. "So we have yet another party at play here? I thought we were chasing after the Emperor Plotmeny's plots against his wife,"

"And that is actually what I thought too," a woman said behind them, her voice echoing off the smooth walls.

Alexender went to point his sword at her chest but he didn't because she was wearing the bright white and golden armour of the Emperor's Regent.

They were looking at the Emperor's Daughter and that only meant one thing.

This was about to get a lot more complicated than Alexender ever thought possible.

CHAPTER 7

"Lady Jasmine," I said, "it is a pleasure to meet you again,"

Out of everything that I had been expecting to happen on this little adventure, it certainly hadn't been that, because Lady Jasmine might have been a good woman, a great socialist and a great champion for the poorer members of her father's empire.

But she was still her father's daughter.

I didn't even bother stepping closer to her as she carefully came into the throne room. Her footsteps echoed loudly off the smooth black walls, and even the black suits of armour against the walls were shaking a little.

I could feel sexy Alexender getting a little closer to me, and I wanted nothing more than for him to come so close to me that I could feel his warm body against mine. But that sadly wasn't going to happen yet.

Maxine placed her hand by her sword and I subtly shook my hand. Jasmine might have been someone I had issues with at times, but I didn't want to hurt her. That would be wrong and a crime against the Goddess.

Jasmine's eyes were focused on me and she didn't smile or frown. She was trying to remain as emotionless as ever, but I could sense she was confused and even a little scared of me. It was probably because I was meant to be dead, she would have wanted that considering she considered me "an extremist" when it came to improving the lives of my subjects.

I just said I did everything I possibly could to better their lives, and my people loved me for it. Of course before they were all mindlessly murdered by Azrael.

Jasmine stopped a few steps from me and she moved both hands down to her two long white swords. She wasn't going to use them, I doubted she was *that* stupid but this was all power and politics.

She probably wanted me to know that she had power here and I wasn't technically a Lady anymore. That was why I had made her come to me, because I wasn't moving for some second-rate Lady, and I wanted her to respect me.

"You were meant to be dead," Jasmine said.

"It is amazing what the Deities will offer you in exchange for becoming their Will Incarnate," I said not wanting to hide the truth from her, and the world.

Jasmine laughed. "You do not believe in the Gods or Goddesses. You do not believe in anything except your own extremist views about righteousness,"

I smiled as that was what the Goddess specialized in, but I didn't want to waste time with someone like Jasmine. I needed information and I wanted to save the lives of the innocent people of this City.

"What do you know about this?" Alexander asked gesturing to the thrones.

Jasmine rolled her eyes. "Not a lot. My father wanted me to assassinate Barabara and Maric for crimes against the Throne so I had to kill the guards that left the city moments ago,"

I nodded. That explained what happened to the guards that stormed out moments before we arrived, so they were probably dead now.

"And I killed them," Jasmine said, "then I made my way here. I had heard reports of some people from the Tanoian Empire passing a border patrol. I did not suspect it to be you,"

I stepped forward. "Why are you here besides the assassination? Your father would not allow an assassination to happen without good reason,"

"Really?" Jasmine asked. "What makes

you qualified to judge my father? The man that helped your own father through tough times with his disastrous policies that allowed hundreds of your citizens to die. And then his high and mighty daughter abandons our country,"

I frowned. Is that what happened? I almost looked away from Jasmine for a moment but I didn't. That would have been a sign of weakness and I couldn't allow that for now, and she was wrong anyway.

"I never abandoned your country," I said. "I send ship after ship and trade carriages after carriages to your empire in the early days of my rule. They were all turned away by your father,"

"No they weren't," Jasmine said grinning. "I ordered them to be turned away and my father aligned himself with more… extreme people,"

I whipped out my swords. "What did you have him do?"

Jasmine smiled. "Lady Barabara has some interesting friends in the Traders' Guild. None that work for your friend Azrael but very interesting characters. I allow their slavers, traders and murderers free rein on the lesser places of my country and they give my father whatever he wants,"

"Heretic!" I shouted.

This was outrageous. Jasmine was an unholy abomination that was allowing and encouraging people to abuse, hurt and kill others for no reason at all. She was a heretic and this was a crime against the Goddess.

My eyes glowed golden.

"I do not know the witch or men who took your target but I know where to start," Jasmine said. "You can kill me all you want but you need me for now,"

I laughed because I was going to put that to the test.

I focused all the Goddess's magic, power and influence on Jasmine and I borrowed into her mind.

"Tell me everything you know about my mission and Azrael,"

Jasmine smiled. "You have no power little Goddess,"

I stomped my foot against the ground, making a loud horrible echo off the smooth walls, and I just hated that she was right. I just couldn't use my influencing power and that was just bloody annoying.

"Stop trying to read my mind," Jasmine said to Maxine.

"It looks like we need her after all," Alexender said a little more delighted than I would have liked.

I just shook my head and put my swords away. I would kill Jasmine because she was committing crimes against the Goddess but Alexender was right. We needed her for now.

But as soon as Maric was dead Jasmine was going to die too.

And that wasn't a threat. It was a promise.

CHAPTER 8

Two hours later, Alexender tied his horse up to a solid marble pole in the middle of the Plotmeny Capital City after Jasmine had led the lead. Alexender was disgusted by how different, shiny and great this capital was compared to the villages and towns they had ridden through on the way here.

Alexender stroked the soft mane of his horse as he focused on all the tall men and women and children in their fine silk robes.

They were all laughing, smiling and the children were skipping about like they didn't have a care in the world.

Everyone was going up and down the long marble road that led from the city gates right to the dark black castle where the Emperor lived. Alexender really liked the small wooden and metal market stalls that lined the entire route.

He was rather impressed at the impressive range of gadgets, jewellery and other beautiful items that were on sale. Alexender hadn't seen any poor people here, any beggars and no signs that they were even allowed in the city.

Maybe the poor were kicked out and forced to live in one of the horrible towns and villages a few miles from here. That was flat out outrageous and disgusting and Alexender hated the Plotmeny Empire if that was true.

Alexender shook the idea away. He only hated the idea because it reminded him too much of his damn home village. He was going to have to talk to Ithane later on about it, but he hated how the cruelty and the harsh reality of living in absolute poverty just wasn't changing fast enough for him.

"This way," Jasmine said.

Alexender went to touch Ithane's waist as he followed Jasmine in her bright white and gold armour, but he forced himself not to. He had only meant it as a friendly gesture saying he would protect her no matter what, but he didn't want to push any boundaries with her. He was meant to protect her, not do her.

He followed as Ithane walked closely next to Jasmine as she took all of them up the marble road towards the castle.

"Do you trust Ithane not to kill her before we find Maric?" Maxine asked.

"I don't know," Alexender said meaning every word of it.

Normal people might have thought the two powerful women were simply walking next to each other, but Alexender could see the subtle glances, the intense focus and the constant watching of the other. Alexender didn't doubt Jasmine was going to try and kill them for some reason, and Ithane would just do the same in the name of the Goddess.

A concept Alexender was still learning how he felt about.

"Just watch them and make sure they don't do anything they'll regret, I don't want a murder to happen," Alexender said to Maxine.

"But I can't read their minds. Ithane is protected by the Goddess and Jasmine... I don't know,"

Alexender nodded his thanks to a young boy as he almost ran into him.

"Let's be careful whatever happens," Alexender said,

"This way," Jasmine said turning left.

Alexender smiled as he followed her down a long narrow side street filled with amazing cafes and small fires with saucepans of boiling oil. There were so many sellers here making crispy doughnuts, sweet fried pastries and the richly spiced cakes he used to love as a kid with his-

Alexender pushed the thought away. It seemed the world wanted him to go back to his home village and that terrified him a lot more than he ever wanted to admit.

"Where are you taking us?" Alexender asked.

"Just here," Jasmine said stopping beside a small elderly woman who was hunched over a pan of boiling hot oil.

Alexender shivered and felt like something

was seriously wrong about the woman, but he couldn't put his finger on it.

The elderly woman poured some vanilla batter into the pan and Alexender just grinned as the air was filled with amazing hints of vanilla, cinnamon and sugar.

"What you want?" the elderly woman asked over the hissing of the oil.

Jasmine folded her arms. "A witch and three men kidnapped Lady Barabara and an outsider today,"

"Good riddance. That old bitch was a nightmare,"

Alexender smiled. He had a feeling he was going to like this woman.

Ithane nodded. "That is one way to describe her, but it is the outsider I am interested in. He's a very bad man that has to be stopped,"

The elderly woman turned over her fried batter and she stared at Ithane.

"A Goddess sent you here," the elderly woman said smiling. "Oh the Gods smile upon me today, and yes I know what you want,"

Alexender watched the elderly woman go over to her little stall and she grabbed a small red leather notebook.

"She listens a lot," Jasmine said. "She was one of my father's top spies before she retired and resulted to this so-called work,"

"Was forced out you mean," the elderly woman said coming back over. "Here,"

Alexender went over to Ithane and Maxine joined him as the woman handed Ithane the notebook.

Ithane grinned. "Midnight you were selling doughnuts to a young couple and overheard a conversation in the distance about a kidnapping. The word *Druidison* was repeated,"

"How did you hear a conversation so far away?" Maxine asked.

Alexender laughed as he realised the elderly woman was a lowkey witch herself. He almost wanted to tell himself off for not noticing it sooner, some Witchfinder he was, but he didn't. He was great at finding rogue witches, not little old ladies.

"I have no idea what that means," Jasmine said.

Ithane shook her head. "That doesn't matter because our Witchfinder will do the rest himself,"

Alexender wasn't exactly sure about that because all the clues were back at the castle, and they had had to leave the castle under Jasmine's so-called authority. Yet Alexender was sure he could find them.

He would just need a little time.

Something he was fairly sure was running out a lot faster than he wanted.

CHAPTER 9

For the next few hours, I had to admit that I flat out loved watching beautiful, sexy Alexander work his own magic on the problem of the witch. As soon as the elderly woman had given us the Druidison clue, Alexander had set off to the nearest library, he had researched and read a whole bunch of ancient texts.

He hadn't found anything.

Then he got back to the castle at full-speed (mainly to piss off Jasmine, or maybe that was my reason for joining him) and he had picked up the witch's magical trace. And we had searched the rest of the city for about an hour before realising the witch could teleport.

And she had teleported back to the capital city, which was where I was now without sexy Alexander as him and Maxine were searching a particular district of the capital city for our target. Apparently, Alexander thought it was better if I spoke to Jasmine more and try not to kill her in the process.

I had no idea why everyone thinks it is so hard for me not to want to kill her. She might be a monster who allowed abusers, slavers and murderers to target her own damn people but I am not a killer in turn.

But Jasmine will die for her crimes against her people, me and the Goddess.

"You seem different these days," Jasmine said.

I was leaning against the back of a brown heavy dining chair in one of the castle's many chambers, focusing on the crackling, roaring fire in front of me.

I had pulled out the dining chair earlier so I could watch the fire and not have to look at Jasmine's heretical face. Not that it worked for too long. The old hag just did the same and sat next to me.

The entire chamber itself was nice enough and I hated it because it had been built on the broken backs of the poor people she was meant to be protecting. I could hear the psychic hisses and cries of the builders as they were killed pushing the immense grey chunks of rock into place.

"Different how?" I asked.

"You mean more confident and more righteousness these days," Jasmine said standing up. "Maybe your Goddess changed you and your mind when she brought you back,"

"That is possible considering she infused me with a portion of herself," I said not really caring what the Goddess might or might not have done to me.

I stood up myself and focused on Jasmine. She was still wearing her bright white and gold armour and I realised there weren't any guards about or servants. No one to stop us if she wanted a fight.

"Why did you want Alexander to tell me to talk to you? It makes no sense, you say you want Maric and Lady Barbara dead but you don't let me go hunting them,"

Jasmine placed a hand on her swords.

"In fact," I said, "ever since we met you're been eyeing me up almost like you're trying to make a decision,"

I moved my own hands down to my swords just in case.

Jasmine frowned and then rolled her eyes. "Fine then, I'll tell you,"

I was surprised by the sheer amount of fear, concern and dread that was in her voice.

She came over to me. "I didn't want to talk in front of the others but something's happened in this castle. I think someone plots to murder my father. I thought it was someone in the Trader's Guilds hence why I allowed them into my empire,"

"It isn't your Empire," I said.

Jasmine laughed. "The Emperor hasn't been well for a few months back. Some kind of fever that isn't going away no matter what magic or herbs or drugs we use,"

I stepped closer, because this was starting to sound a lot more like the work of Azrael, but he always killed and assassinated heads of state quickly. He never drew back the process from what little I knew about him.

"I've been running the Empire from

behind the scenes and it's why my father never gave the assassination order. He would never do anything about Lady Barbara so I acted before she could,"

"That makes a lot more sense," I said pacing about.

Alexander had been right about the Emperor not wanting to kill his wife, and my own blindness to the horrible woman that the pretend Lady was had blinded that information to me. It made sense that Lady Barabara would want to work with Azrael now to kill Jasmine and then take over the Plotmeny Empire when the Emperor died of this illness.

And I was willing to bet the only reason why the Emperor wasn't dead yet was because Azrael didn't command it.

I was about to reply when my skin turned icy cold and I felt the Goddess touching my soul.

A simple image of Alexender formed in my mind and I just knew that he was in danger and I had to save him.

I didn't know how I knew but I knew the Goddess was going to allow me to teleport so I clicked my wrists and a massive golden portal opened.

"With me!" I shouted to Jasmine as I stormed through the portal.

Just hoping beyond hope that I could save the man I was seriously falling for.

CHAPTER 10

The rich warming aromas of bitter coffee, sweet caramel and delicious crispy pastries filled the air as Alexander took out his sword and went into a small, damp living room. The smooth walls were covered in small burn patterns made from years upon years of boiling oil bubbling up and splattering, and the hard wooden floors hardly looked much better.

Alexender was glad he had managed to track this particular witch throughout the entire city, and she had clearly prepared for a Witchfinder. She had gone all over the city and inside tons of little magical places in an effort to make him lose her scent.

Alexender had to admit she was clever but he was a Witchfinder and he was going to find her no matter what.

The living room was hardly filled with much furniture, which concerned Alexender more than he wanted to admit. There was only a horrible boiling cauldron of oil and a large metal rack filled with freshly fried doughnuts.

"This place looks *interesting*," Maxine said.

Alexender smiled. As much as Alexender loved the wonderful smell, it was strange that a witch would want to be cooking doughnuts after kidnapping a pretend Lady and Maric. He supposed the kidnapped idiots needed to eat as much as the next person, but doughnuts were an odd choice.

Alexender went over to the metal rack. "You want to try one?"

"No thank you," Maxine said coming over too. "They might be cursed or something,"

Alexender nodded. That was exactly why he wasn't touching them, it didn't matter how great and crispy and fluffy they looked. Alexander really did not want to try one, because Maxine was probably right.

He held his hand over them and closed his eyes. He wasn't sure how his "imagery" magic worked but he was hoping his magic would let him see something.

A moment later images of people laughing

and smiling and eating the doughnuts filled his mind. Then the images were burnt away and replaced with people vomiting up their own stomachs, guts and small rat-like creatures were crawling out of their throats.

Alexender took a few steps back and thrusted out his hands. Torrents of white fire shot out of them turning the doughnuts to ash.

"They were cursed," Alexander said.

Maxine folded her arms. "So we have a kidnapped Lady and servant of Azrael. We have an Emperor wanting to take revenge on his wife, and we have a witch wanting to poison innocent people,"

"None of it makes sense," Alexender said really wanting a break in this adventure. "Is it possible the kidnapping and our mission aren't connected?"

"No," Maxine said walking about the living room. "Why would Lady Barabara be taken the same day we come to investigate and the Emperor's forces come to do something?"

Alexender supposed she had a good point. He still didn't like it because nothing was adding up here, and he had no idea who this witch was working for. And as much as he wanted to believe a random witch wanted to kidnap a pretend Lady and Maric, he seriously doubted it.

That sort of power move came from someone with power, influence and money. A random witch didn't have any of them.

"Oh crap," Maxine said.

Alexender whipped out his sword on instinct. "What?"

"We've been thinking about this all wrong and damn Jasmine gave us all the information we needed earlier,"

Alexender shrugged. He was clearly not seeing something.

"Jasmine allowed the Traders Guild to allow traders, slavers and murderers into the Plotmeny Empire in exchange for giving the Emperor whatever he wanted,"

Alexander felt a chill run down his spine.

"And who else would have the power and influence to want to take out a Lady, a servant of Azrael- a criminal mastermind I doubt the Guild is happy about- and where is the Emperor by the way?"

Alexender nodded. He should have seen it sooner because it was weird the Emperor hadn't met with Ithane. She was still an extremely attractive noble and the Emperor would have wanted to meet with her.

Unless he wasn't about anymore to do just that.

"If the Traders Guild is behind this," Alexander said, "then that means they've been playing an extreme long game with the Plotmeny Empire,"

Maxine looked into the boiling cauldron. "They get their agents into the Empire without restraint, then they deal with the Emperor and kidnap two powerful enemies. That is clever,"

"And now they want to murder innocent people," Alexander said. "No wonder the Goddess brought us here or at least didn't stop us coming here,"

Maxine hissed. "We have to warn Ithane now because Jasmine has to be involved,"

Alexender went to head to the door when the boiling hot oil exploded out the cauldron.

Raining down on them.

Alexender collapsed to the floor screaming out in agony.

The oil burnt his flesh.

And Alexander saw a witch crawl out of

the cauldron.

She was going to kill them.

CHAPTER 11

As soon as my massive golden portal dropped me and Jasmine into the horrible living room filled with marks of burning oil on its walls and floor I saw the witch.

I hated her. I could tell she was a foul abomination that had to die. I could sense how she killed, murdered and mutilated innocent people and that was a crime against the Goddess I could never allow to go unpunished.

I felt the wonderful warm of the Goddess fill me and my eyes burnt golden and my skin glowed. My golden armour radiated holy energy and I loved how my swords caught on cleansing fire.

I was going to slaughter the witch.

"Help," Maxine said.

I wanted to shout out in pain as I saw Maxine roll around on the floor screaming and crying and hissing. The burns were awful on her and now the witch had to die.

I couldn't bear to look at sexy Alexender.

I flew at the witch.

Her black robes swirled around her sickly thin body. She screamed at me.

The air crackled with magical energy.

Boiling hot oil flew at me.

It touched my skin.

I didn't feel anything. The Goddess was protecting me.

I leapt into the air.

The witch thrusted out her hands.

I flew to one side.

Smashing into a wall.

The witch charged at me.

I rolled out the way.

She moved rapidly.

She punched me.

Kicked me.

Headbutted me.

I leapt up.

Thrusting out my hands.

White holy fire shot out of them.

The witch screamed in agony. Her robe caught alight.

She thrusted out both her hands.

Black lightning shot out.

I ducked.

I charged forward.

The lightning hit me.

I screamed.

Every muscle fiber in my body felt like it was being ripped apart.

Jasmine charged forward.

The witch clicked her fingers stopping the lightning.

Jasmine flew backwards.

I charged.

Swinging my swords.

The witch tried to react.

She was too slow.

I swung.

My swords chomped into the flesh.

My eyes glowed golden and the witch exploded into ash.

I immediately went over to Maxine and beautiful Alexender and held a hand over both of them as the wonderful Goddess healed them both.

Alexender was the first to get up and then he looked like he was going to hug me. I wanted nothing more than for him to wrap his strongly manly, sexy arms around me and me tight. I wanted that so badly.

But he went for a bloody hand shake of all things and that was broken a moment later when Maxine pointed her sword at Jasmine's throat.

"What's going on?" I asked coming over to Jasmine.

I might not have liked the woman but I wasn't going to allow her to die, yet.

"The Traders Guilds are involved," Alexender said. "We found out just moments before that witch attacked us,"

I nodded. That made so much sense. Who else in the entire world would have the power, influence and cunning to kidnap Barabara, plan to assassinate the Emperor and kidnap so many people from the City of Barabara.

"And you allowed them into your Empire," I said to Jasmine.

She frowned. "I didn't mean to, honest. I did not want any of this to happen but they poisoned my father. I had to save him. I had to do-"

I waved her silent and took out my sword pressing it slightly against her throat.

"You endangered the lives of your people, the people you are meant to protect and the people you are meant to serve," I said. "You have not only failed them, but you have failed as a human being, a good person and you have failed the Goddess,"

I wanted so badly to kill Jasmine. She was a foul monster that had brought so much pain and suffering to her subjects but I had a feeling I was going to need her a little longer.

"I am not sorry about that," Jasmine said. "I don't care what your Goddess said but the Guild poisoned my father and I was just trying to save him. What would you do for your father?"

I grinned because that was a pointless question. She knew my father had died of cancer five years ago and I had done everything I could to save him within reason, and I certainly didn't try to sell my own people to slavers, abusers and murderers to save him.

There were limits.

"What do you know about this entire damn thing?" I asked. "You have to know something else about the kidnapping,"

Jasmine looked at Alexender. "You found the witch so you can find something else that will help you,"

I looked at Alexender and smiled. "What do you need him to find?"

I lowered my sword and gestured Jasmine to stand up.

"The Guild has a single operative, a Council Regent, in the Empire and he loves archaic knowledge and he seeks the Lirus Operatius or Book of Operatives to be more precise and to translate. Find that book and the Guild will do whatever you command,"

I gestured Alexender and Maxine to come over to me. I doubted Jasmine was going to run but it didn't matter if she did, she would die at some point.

"What is this Book of Operatives?" Maxine asked.

I frowned. "It's an ancient text from this part of the world that focuses on machines like self-driving carriages, how to control dragons and how to build steamships or whatever they're called. Even steamplanes, whatever they are,"

"So whoever controls it, controls modern warfare I presume," Alexender said.

I nodded. "I do not trust the Guild with such information and I do not trust Jasmine with it either,"

"Hey!" she said.

I ignored her. "The Book is easily a thousand years old but I did read a Newsparchment article four years ago about it being discovered and sold to a fellow Noble,"

"Who?" Maxine asked.

"Well," I said laughing, "Lady Barabara springs to mind,"

"Oh," the other two said.

I turned around to ask if Jasmine knew where all the Lady's stuff was but she was gone.

She had escaped and now I was certainly going to kill her at the end of this adventure, because she was a monster and an affront to the work of the Goddess.

But first we had to find this book because as much as I didn't want to admit it thousands of lives might depend on it.

No pressure then.

No pressure at all.

CHAPTER 12

Alexander was seriously impressed with how brilliantly Ithane could fight, heal and figure out all the things that he couldn't do alone. She was just such a hot, fit, powerful woman that he really was starting to love more and more each day. He wasn't sure if there was anything she couldn't actually do.

It was even better when Ithane had tapped into the Goddess's power and she had found out where Lady Barabra used to stay when she rarely came into the City.

Alexander carried a large pile of old dusty leather-bound books over to an equally dusty brown oak table. Ithane was sitting at one end and poor Maxine was snoring away at the mid-point of the table. Alexander had already grabbed her pile of books and he was more than happy to let her sleep.

Alexander wasn't sure if Ithane needed sleep anymore but he certainly wasn't going to stay up too much later. And if he slept he wouldn't have to keep thinking about his damn home village.

"I used to have a little villa like this," Ithane said from the other end of the table. "I used to love it in the summer,"

Alexander smiled. He loved hearing about Ithane's childhood and he could understand why she liked it here. Lady Barabara had tons of different books on the floor-to-ceiling blue bookcases on every single topic he could imagine.

There was a beautiful chandelier overhead and the two immense windows that they had opened to their left allowed a wonderful view of the capital at night. Alexander really liked all the lights, small fires and little buildings in the distance. Even the gentle mutterings of the people outside was rather calming.

"What's been on your mind though since the twisted forest? I know you mentioned the thing about your home village, but... I don't know. You need to talk about it,"

"No thanks," Alexander said.

He grabbed a heavy dusty book off the top of the pile and started skim-reading it for any mention of the Book of Operatives.

"Actually," Alexander said annoyed he was changing his mind, "what do you know about Montoney?"

"Not a lot," Ithane said flicking through a book, "I know it's a village on the other side of the world. It used to be the global centre of fishing exports but that was about two hundred years ago,"

Alexender was seriously impressed. She was beautiful, an amazing fighter and really intelligent. He was certain there was nothing she couldn't do now.

"I grew up there," Alexender said hating that fact.

Maxine snored loudly for a moment but snuffled again.

Alexender laughed. "Bless her. But Montoney is a shithole these days and it's still a fishing village but it's controlled by barons and his enforcers, and yeah not nice,"

Ithane slammed a book closed and took out another book.

"What was it like growing up there?" Ithane asked not liking the idea of barons and enforcers. "Did you get any freedom or whatnot?"

Alexender frowned. "They got all the children to work in the docks as soon as they were old enough to run and then the older children had to carry heavy boxes of fish whenever the boats came in. I broke my foot once when a box dropped on it. My brother was killed when a friend dropped a box on him. He was two years younger,"

Alexender really hated this damn situation, he hated his childhood, he hated his village and he hated the bastard barons.

"Fucking hell. I'm so sorry that sounds… I'm sorry," Ithane said hating the barons and village. "I had no idea. We can change the subject if you want,"

Alexender shook his head as he closed his current book because it was a cooking book, not the Book of Operatives.

"It's okay. It's just the village is in danger and I need to make a decision by tomorrow night about whether I go and save the village or not. What do you think?"

"You know what I'm going to say,"

Alexender smiled. "Well yeah, you're going to say that innocent people are in danger and that is reason enough to go. You're also going to say that Azrael is focusing on the village so we have to go,"

"Exactly," Ithane said closing another book.

"But it's… I'm not exactly welcome there after I escaped, the Barons are foul and… there's a lot of bad memories wrapped up there,"

Ithane stopped reading. "What do you mean *escaped*?"

Alexender shivered and stood up and then sat back down again. He just looked at beautiful Ithane and focused on her long blond hair and her glowing skin. He loved her and he felt safe around her.

He could tell her anything.

Alexender took a deep breathe. "The entire village was surrounded by brutes and guards. If anyone tried to escape, they would be crippled by the brutes. My grandmother tried once and her legs were broken so many times she was wheelchair bound for the rest of her life,"

"Goddess," Ithane said.

"So I wanted to escape so I made a deal with a girl, well young woman actually. She was how I lost my virginity and all that. We promised we could escape together because she was pregnant and we could run away together,"

Ithane moved uncomfortably in her seat.

Alexender smiled weakly. "So the day came, it was early morning and we ran for it.

We caused an explosion in the middle of town to distract the guards and we ran,"

"Clever,"

Alexander shook his head. "No, because the brutes chased us. We were only 18 so we dodged them and fled but they fired a crossbow. My girlfriend had a bolt through the knee, she begged me to go on without her and I…"

Ithane stood up and came over to him.

Alexander didn't even care anymore. He just hugged Ithane and flat out loved the great feeling of her warm body against his.

"And I promised I would come back for her. I ran and climbed and jumped over the village walls as fast as I could. All whilst I listened to her screaming and crying and I kept running,"

Alexander buried his face into Ithane's neck and he hated how he was shaking. He had loved Elizabeth so damn much and he had left her. He had left her to be killed, murdered or Goddess knows what.

"Elizabeth could be alive or dead and I don't know," Alexander said.

Ithane gently stroked him on the back of his head. Alexander laughed because he felt like a small child but he loved Ithane touching him.

"There's nothing you could have done," Ithane said. "And you know I want us to go back in the name of the Goddess, but maybe you need to deal with the past,"

Alexander shook his head. That couldn't be right, it just couldn't be right.

Ithane sadly broke the hug. "But that is a choice for you and you alone. Just know that me and Maxine will be with you whatever you decide,"

"Exactly," Maxine said looking over one of Ithane's books. "And this might help us. I know where the Book of Operatives is,"

CHAPTER 13

The next morning, the thick aromas of incense, burning sage and charred flesh filled the air as me, beautiful Alexander and Maxine went into a massive white ivory tower a few kilometres outside the capital city.

The inside of the immense tower was easily the size of two football pitches (an awful game if there ever was one) with tens upon tens of short men and women dressed in dirty white robes. They were all carrying books, parchments and so-called holy objects to the other Gods and Goddesses.

No one even batted us an eyelid.

"What's the plan?" Maxine asked.

I shivered a little as I realised that whilst most of the so-called holy objects like the golden plates, bowls and jewel-encrusted daggers, weren't actually holy. There were a few items somewhere that were filled with holy power.

"Can you read their minds?" I asked. "Let us see what they know about the Book of Operatives,"

Maxine laughed. "Ithane, my magic doesn't work like that. I can only read their minds for what they're thinking right now,"

I nodded. It was worth a try but I felt a pressure start to press against my mind like someone was slowly starting to inflate a ballon inside my skull. Whatever these holy objects were, they clearly didn't agree with me.

I took a few steps forward and then everyone stopped what they were doing and they stared at us.

No one blinked. No one moved. No one breathed.

After a moment all the men and women moved a little and placed whatever they were carrying on one of the massive oak tables that lined the middle of the tower's entrance.

"Hello," they all said as one.

It was damn creepy and I gasped as I saw their veins were black, their eyes were bloodshot and I realised exactly what those holy objects were.

"The God of Betrayal, Murder and Annihilation," I said. "I should have known you would have found a way to stop me again,"

All the men and women laughed as one.

I heard Maxine and Alexender whip out their swords and I did the same.

"Do not be scared Lady Tano," they all said. "You seek the Book of Operatives as do I, it is here because I can feel it but I struggle to find its exact location. Help out an old friend shall you?"

I shook my head. "You are a murderer, a betrayer and you caused me to lose everything,"

All the men and women took a few steps closer and shook their heads. "Never, I did not do anything to your Empire. That was all Azrael and I want him as dead as you do. Let us work together,"

Maxine stepped forward. "So you can kill us and make us betray each other?"

"Feast on them!" they all shouted.

"Goddess defend us," I said.

I didn't feel any warmth, power or divine energy fill my body. My Goddess had left me and abandoned me. I shook the stupid idea from my mind because that was impossible.

The Goddess was testing me and I was going to pass.

I charged forward.

Swinging my swords.

Slicing into flesh.

Chomping into chests.

Cutting off heads.

Maxine stormed forward.

Swinging and killing as she went.

Alexender leapt over me.

He lashed. Slashed. Killed.

Black blood sprayed up walls.

Shards of bone littered the floor.

There were too many.

They pushed us back.

More corrupted men were coming from behind.

There were too many.

I needed help. I needed my Goddess. I needed my power.

I charged forward.

Swinging. Lashing. Swirling my blade.

I killed as many as I could.

Hands gripped my shoulders.

Pulling me down.

I collapsed to the floor.

I heard Alexender scream.

Maxine shrieked.

My friends were dying. I had to protect them. They were innocent.

I had to do something.

I went to swing my sword. There wasn't enough room to get momentum.

I screamed out in terror.

A deafening roar ripped through the tower.

Something exploded. The entire tower shook.

Extreme heat filled the tower's entrance.

The enemy screamed as they melted all

around us.

I stood up and just frowned as I saw three muscular men coming towards me, Maxine and Alexender. And standing right in the doorway was a woman I had only heard about and I had hoped beyond hope I would never have to meet.

Georgia The Blood Queen, The Witch Who Killed a Thousand Men In Ten Seconds.

Not exactly someone I want to meet in a dark alley let alone right after a battle.

CHAPTER 14

Alexender rubbed his wrists as one of the dumb, stupid, pathetic muscular men in his foul armour undid his handcuffs. Alexender looked over at beautiful Ithane and he was seriously impressed that she didn't even react to her red-raw wrists as her own handcuffs were removed. Maxine hissed in pain.

He was certain now that nothing phased Ithane, and it only made him like her even more (if such a thing was possible).

Alexender went to adjust his heavy solid-pine chair and move it closer to the small coffee table in front of them, but he didn't dare move in case Georgia thought he was going to attack her.

"It's a very nice place here. I see you have cabinets, chairs and tables made by my Empire," Ithane said.

Alexender supposed she had a good point because the little "hotel" or office room they were in was rather stylish, even for somewhere in the capital. The coffee table looked brand-new, never-used and expensive as did the tall glass cabinets filled with books and relics that lined the walls.

"Thank you Lady Tano," Georgia said. "I am glad to see you doing so good,"

Alexender actually looked at Georgia for the first time and truly looked. He had only heard of her, her work and how evil she was whenever someone hired her. And she was beyond beautiful with her high cheekbones, long brown hair that looked so lifeful and thick, he was almost jealous of it.

Georgia's bronze armour was a strange combination of maybe four different designs, one from each corner of the world, and Alexender couldn't help but admit. Maybe that was why it was rumoured, no one had or could harm her. Even golden lions on the shoulder pads were a little odd but they were stylish and suited her.

Georgia turned to Alexender. "And how comes I have never met the great Witchfinder Alexender Quill before? I would have thought you would have been offered a contract or two for me,"

Alexender smiled. He had been offered tons of contracts to find her, kill her and bring the person her head back for even more money. But Alexender had always refused the contracts because Georgia was a little out of his league. And Alexender hated using his magic to kill too much to take on a case where he would *have* to use it to kill.

Magic just shouldn't be used to kill.

"You are too boring for me," Alexender said.

Georgia laughed. "The Traders Guild did not say that when they hired me to deal with Lady Barabara and Maric and Azrael. And no, before you idiots ask I do not know who Azrael is,"

Alexender rolled his eyes because that

information would have been nice.

"Then why bring us here?" Maxine asked her eyes glowing subtly.

Maxine screamed out in pain and Georgia laughed a little. Alexender really wished Maxine wouldn't try out her mind-reading magic on extremely powerful witches. It never ended well.

"I have brought you here because we have been fooled," Georgia said clicking her fingers and a golden leather-bound book floated over to the coffee table.

Alexender had never seen such a beautiful book that was so thick and covered in so much detail. There were thousands of symbols, carvings and equations on the book cover alone. Alexender had no idea how many were inside.

Ithane frowned. "We didn't have to find the book to get leverage on you,"

Georgia nodded. "You didn't even know I was the woman in charge of the Traders Guild here, did you?"

"No," Alexender said wanting to make a play. "But we know your plan to kill the Emperor,"

"Of course," Georgia said. "The Emperor will die once the God of Betrayal, Murder and Annihilation decides the Guild's business is done here,"

Alexender stood up and felt two massive hands grip his shoulders and force him back down.

Ithane stood up and Alexender smiled as her eyes glowed golden and muscular men backed away from her.

"You make a bargain with a Dark God," Ithane said her voice barely managing to contain her anger.

Alexander really didn't want that anger to be turned on him.

"How dare you consort with Gods and Goddesses that seek to kill innocent people," Ithane said. "Do you not realise how many people are suffering because of you?"

"Profit and loss is all my Masters care about, and I am on the Guild Council you realise. No one is more powerful than me. Not even Heads of State or Ladies. I control the flow of goods, I control the flow of money, I control the flow of illegal items that countries depend on,"

Alexender laughed. Georgia really was stupid.

"What's so funny?" Georgia asked.

Alexender leant forward. "You do realise you are in the presence of the Will incarnate of a deity. I think Ithane is a little higher than you, both morally and in power,"

Georgia stood up, clicked her fingers and a long crystal staff appeared.

"I will give you one choice. You can leave now and never return. You will allow me and the Guild to continue our operations of claiming the Plotmeny Empire for ourselves, or you will die," Georgia said.

Alexender and Maxine stood up at the exact same time.

"You are the one that will die," Ithane said her eyes glowing bright gold.

"Not right now," Georgia said raising her staff.

Alexender grabbed Ithane and Maxine and raced out the door.

Georgia slammed her staff on the ground.

Alexender leapt down the wooden staircase as the room exploded.

Alexender didn't even bother checking if

Georgia and the three men were still alive. They would be and now they were free to speed up their plans.

And Alexender had a feeling that Ithane was going to want to kill them more and ever.

And Alexender didn't have a problem with that.

Not a problem at all.

CHAPTER 15

I seriously couldn't believe how much sense this was making now and how much I wanted to slaughter that heretical, evil Georgia and those three men. Of course, the problem was still only she knew where Lady Barabara and Maric where so I couldn't kill her without losing the information. A problem for later for sure.

But with someone as powerful and evil as Georgia in charge of this operation, it made perfect sense how she could infiltrate the Plotmeny Empire, promise (with some magical persuasion I am sure) Jasmine and the Plotmeny Government to allow the Guild's abusers and murders and slavers into the Empire, and then Georgia could do whatever she wanted. She probably had the magical power to bend anyone's mind to her will.

And as for the Emperor, well that was clear as day now, the mystery illness could have been a "gift" created by the God of Betrayal, Murder and Annihilation. Even though I still want to understand what exactly the God promised Georgia and the Guild and in exchange for what.

A lot of answers but certainly more questions.

"What now?" Maxine asked.

I led Alexender and her up towards the massive black castle along the perfectly maintained white marble road and little buildings either side. There were still a ton of wooden and metal market stalls selling all sorts of great items but I had a mission. I hadn't had time to shop.

I stepped out the way of a young family walking past. "Georgia's plan is exposed. She has to kill the Emperor now and make sure the Guild is ready to takeover the Plotmeny Empire properly,"

"But I don't understand how killing the Emperor helps them," Alexender said. "He still has a daughter,"

I shook my head because they still weren't understanding what was happening.

"A witch like Georgia has the power to make anyone do whatever she wants. The dying wish of the Emperor could be to make her the new Empress,"

"Holy shit," Maxine said. "That isn't right,"

I whipped out my swords as a young family coming towards me ran away. Okay, maybe I shouldn't have done that in public.

"That's why we have to kill Georgia and stop the Guild. We cannot suffer a heretic to live," I said surprised how righteous I was being.

Maybe the Goddess was influencing my thoughts more than I wanted to admit but I didn't care.

"Stop," watchmen shouted in their black armour up ahead.

All three of us whipped out our swords as ten Watchmen charged at us. Men and women ran from the street.

I flew forward. I didn't want to kill them.

They were innocent people.

I put my swords away. The others did the same.

The Watchmen whipped out their swords.

They swung their swords.

I ducked. Leapt. Dodged.

I rolled forward.

Jumping up.

Smashing my fists into their heads.

Knocking two of them out cold.

Two down. Eight to go.

Alexender leapt into the air. Kicking two in the head.

Maxine choked one of them. She knocked them out.

Five down. Five to go.

Arrows rained down on us.

I clicked my fingers.

A golden holy shield formed a roof over us. I couldn't see the archers but I really wanted them to fall asleep for two hours.

I felt some warmth fill me. The arrows stopped. Maybe the Goddess did my wish.

The Watchmen flew forward.

These men were quick.

Too quick.

Maxine dodged all them expertly. She was probably reading their minds. The cheat.

I ducked.

I punched.

I kicked.

I blocked.

I leapt forward.

Surprising one of the Watchmen. He fell to the ground. I kicked his head.

Six down.

Maxine choked another one.

Alexender smashed another one over the head.

Nine down. One to go.

The last one screamed. He charged. He swung both his swords.

I could sense his fear. He was going too fast. Too uncontrolled.

He swung at me.

Rapidly.

He was too quick.

A sword sliced my neck.

I shot out my hands.

A fireball engulfed him.

And I just fell to my knees as I heard him scream out in agony as he was burnt alive and he screamed over and over for help until he simply collapsed.

He died within seconds.

I clicked my fingers and I healed my neck wound but I couldn't believe what the hell had just happened. All I had wanted to do was make sure no one died and I had just killed an innocent person.

A man that probably had a partner, a family and maybe some kids. I had just killed someone who was exactly the type of person I claimed to protect at all costs.

"You didn't have a choice," Alexender said placing a loving hand on my shoulder.

I fought back tears because I knew this wasn't *all* my fault but there was always a choice. I could have used my magic differently instead of a deadly reflex reaction, but I hadn't and now someone was dead.

An innocent man was dead.

I forced myself up and I stormed off towards the castle because now I had to kill Georgia because she had sent those Watchmen after us.

And she had sent that poor man to die.

And there was no punishment she

deserved more than death.

CHAPTER 16

Alexander, Ithane and Maxine found Georgia about an hour later inside the immense black castle that laid at the heart of the capital city.

Alexander whipped out his swords as he went into a massive cathedral-like chamber with black marble walls that rose up to create a domed ceiling effect, golden chandeliers hung down and bright golden candlelight lit up the chamber.

Alexander flat out hated how cold, damp and empty the castle was without any guards, any servants and everyone was just gone.

Much like the City of Barabara.

Alexander didn't doubt for a moment that foul Georgia had done something to the people of that city when she had kidnapped Lady Barabara and Maric. And now she was going to pay for it.

Alexander just shook his head as Georgia stood in the middle of the chamber and grinned at them. He hated her strange, ornate armour that made no sense and now he noticed the golden lions had moved from the last time he had seen them.

He heard Ithane move behind him so he spun around and realised the three muscular men were there holding swords.

The men gestured them to go in deeper and Alexander did. Ithane and Maxine did the same.

Alexander looked up at the ceiling as he went closer to Georgia. All his Witchfinder senses were on fire, his skin felt alive and like it was on fire and a pressure was building against his mind. He had never faced power like hers.

"Let the Witch fight the Witchfinder," Georgia said. "And then I will make you watch as I annihilate the ceiling and kill the Emperor,"

Alexander's eyes widened as he realised they were directly under the Emperor's bed chamber. One magical blast would level this chamber, if not the castle and kill them all and the Emperor in the process.

Alexander raised his swords. Sexy Ithane and Maxine did the same.

Georgia shot out her hands.

The two women slammed against the marble walls. Alexander wanted to check if they were okay but he noticed they were being trapped there by some magical force.

He just hoped the Goddess could free them at some point.

"Now let us see the power of a Witchfinder," Georgia said.

She clicked her fingers and the muscular men screamed in agony behind him.

Alexander spun around and he backed away from the men as they collapsed to the ground. The air crackled with magical energy and the men were mutilated and their human forms annihilated.

The men's legs and legs and fingers became claws and talons. Their necks elongated to become longer and narrower. And their faces twisted to become bird-like with razor-sharp teeth perfect for devouring flesh.

The monsters flew at him.

Alexander charged.

He leapt into the air.

He swung.

His sword shattered upon impact.

The monsters crackled.

Their beaks smashed into him.

Sending Alexander flying backwards.

He slammed into a wall.

His vision blurred.

Alexander ran forward.

He couldn't see.

He could barely see shapes.

The monsters crackled around him.

His vision cleared.

He couldn't see any of the monsters.

They dropped down from the ceiling.

Alexander hissed.

The monsters had morphed into a single massive three-headed bird-like monster.

The monster pinned him to the ground.

Pinning his legs under the monster's talons.

Alexander tried to move. Tried to fight. Tried to punch.

He couldn't.

Alexander heard Ithane and Maxine scream out in agony. Georgia was hurting them.

Alexander had to be the unthinkable. He had to use his magic. He had to kill this monster forever.

He stared into the cold eyes of the monster.

Alexander roared.

The air exploded with golden magical light.

The monster shrieked.

It leapt off him.

Alexander jumped up.

He thrusted out his hands.

White fire shot out of them.

Immense torrents flew at the monster.

The monster ran.

It tried to outrun the flames.

The torrents rode towards the monster.

Alexander felt the torrents jerk and take on a life of its own. His magic wanted the monster dead.

The torrents smashed into the monster.

Feathers burnt.

Flesh melted.

Bones popped.

The monster screamed and screamed as it died but Alexander did not stop. He needed to kill this monster so he could focus on Georgia and stop her killing innocent people.

As soon as the monster died Alexander spun around to look at Georgia but she was gone.

Something slammed into the back of his head and his world went black.

CHAPTER 17

I wanted nothing more than to slaughter that bitch as Alexender collapsed to the ground like a lifeless corpse. She was going to pay so dearly for all of this and I hated it as I felt her magic pin me to the awfully cold black marble walls. I hated this chamber.

I was going to destroy it.

Georgia laughed at me as she came over and stood right in front of me.

"Do you feel your Goddess?" Georgia asked. "You won't because the God of Betrayal, Murder and Annihilation is keeping her out. She wants to help you, protect and keep you alive but she cannot,"

"You mock my faith?" I asked knowing Georgia was stupid.

"Your Goddess is weak, pathetic and she has nothing that can help now. She will watch you burn and she will watch as I kill every single last person in this city,"

Her voice was deepening and sounding booming. Almost like her voice wasn't her own anymore or maybe none of Georgia was really herself anymore.

"What did you give up to the God?" I asked.

Georgia cackled over and over as her eyes blackened and her fingers became claws and she ripped out her own heart and threw it on the floor.

"She gave me everything," the thing inside Georgia's body said. "She gave me her power, her mind and her soul so I could corrupt the body,"

Georgia took a deep breath. "You smell that woman, you smell the fear in the air and all the ripe tasty little humans that are on this world,"

I gasped. I knew exactly who this was or what this was. This was a shard of the God's soul and I was in the presence of the God of Betrayal, Murder and Annihilation.

I felt a warmth feel me and I forced myself not to smile because my Goddess was here and I was not alone. She was going to protect me and I was going to end this in her name.

The air crackled with black magical energy.

"The Traders Guild were foolish, Azrael was foolish and everyone else in this world is a fool," the God said.

I clicked my fingers and the magical force holding me and Maxine broke and the God just grinned.

"So little Goddess you are smart enough to avoid my traps. Cast your champion and let me kill her," the God said.

I charged. I whipped out my swords.

My eyes and armour glowed bright gold. I felt the wonderful warmth of my Goddess fill me.

I flew at the God.
I leapt into the air.
I kicked.
Swung.
Punched.
The God dodged all my attacks.
I landed.
I rolled forward.
The God swung his claws at me.
I dodged.
He attacked.
Again.
Again.
Again.
He was so quick. He was a blur.
I relied on instinct.
I blocked. Dodged. Rolled.
Blocked. Dodged. Rolled.
He jumped forward.
Knocking me off balance.
Maxine charged.
He shot out his hands.
Black fire slammed into her.
Sending her flying.
She smashed into a wall.
Knocking her out cold.
I stormed forward.
Smashing into him.
The God flew backwards.
I thrusted out my swords.
White fire shot out of them.
The God absorbed it.
Aiming it upwards.
All my magical power was aimed towards the ceiling.

The castle shook violently as the ceiling

exploded.

I sunk to my knees as the chamber was filled with bright white dust from the ceiling and the room above it.

Little chunks of bone, ash and charred flesh rained down around me and I realised what the hell I had just done.

I had just killed the very man, the very Emperor I had been meaning to protect at all costs.

I had failed myself, the Goddess and all the amazing innocent people of the Plotmeny Empire.

"Well well well," the God said as he magicked up a black sword and pointed it at my throat. "Your Goddess is useless if she can't even protect an Emperor,"

I looked at the God. "She is not weak. She is not pathetic. She is not your downfall,"

The God laughed. "Then who is my downfall?"

"Me," I said.

I swung my sword.

Knocking the God's sword away.

I leapt forward.

Tackling the God to the ground.

I punched him.

Again. Again. Again.

He turned to shadow and floated behind me.

He put me in a headlock.

"One false move and I will snap your neck," the God said.

I hated the damn amusement in his voice. I so badly wanted to kill her.

"I want to see your Goddess. I want her to come down here and I can kill her with my bare hands,"

"Aren't you powerful enough to kill her in your Divine Realm?" I asked not knowing the answer.

He laughed. "Of course I am but she hides too well. She is weak in the Divine Realm until you save and protect so many people that she grows in strength,"

I nodded. I understood now why my Goddess needed me and wanted me to live. She needed me even more than I needed her because without me no one would be saved and it was the act of saving people that gave her strength.

And I would give her some strength now.

I closed my eyes and channelled all my magical power and influence and desire to protect innocent lives at the shard of the God.

The air hummed violently and I asked him a simple question.

"Tell me everything you know about Azrael," I said.

The God staggered back and hissed in agony as my influencing power took hold. He released me from my headlock and he cried out in crippling pain.

I stood up and I punched him in the face.

The God collapsed to the ground and cried as he fought with all his being against my influence. But this wasn't the Divine Realm, this was my Realm and now the God was going to have to play by the rules of reality.

"Azrael is a puppet master of thousands of agents, spies and workers all across the world. He seeks to annihilate the Gods and Goddesses and free will by finding something called the Last Hope Protocol. That is all I know,"

The God cradled his head and his eyes bulged out.

I grabbed my sword and raised it. "Is that

everything?"

"Yes, yes, yes that is all I know I swear!"

"Then your punishment is well overdue heretic," I said.

I swung my sword and I beheaded the God and it turned to ash. It was over but at what cost.

CHAPTER 18

Alexander folded his arms and just shook his head as he stood in the Emperor's bedroom a few hours later, he had no idea what the hell the Emperor had sacrificed or put in place to make the God and Georgia believe he was in his chambers when he wasn't, but Alexander really didn't care.

He leant against a wonderfully warm statue of a naked woman as he watched beautiful Ithane sit on the edge of the Emperor's massive bed with golden bedframe, golden silk sheets and more stuffed animals than Alexander wanted to see.

Ithane had been sitting next to the coughing Emperor for a few minutes muttering some words that Alexander flat didn't understand. They were clearly a different language but Alexander had no idea which one.

Alexander smiled at Maxine as she came back into the immense secondary bedchamber with a short line of male and female servants in red robes carrying food, water and fresh linens for the Emperor. Alexander really liked seeing them all smile and they looked like they were genuinely pleased to see the Emperor.

Maybe the Emperor was a great person to work for after all.

The sweet aromas of burning sage, cinnamon and oranges filled the bed chamber and Alexander was really enjoying the wonderful taste of orange tarts like his mother used to make form on his tongue.

Alexander rolled his eyes. He only had a few hours left to make a decision about whether or not he was going home to save his village. As much as he didn't want to go because of the past, he just knew it was his duty to go and save as many people as possible. He might have dreamt or actually overheard the conversation between the so-called shard of a God and Ithane earlier. But if saving innocent people gave the Goddess strength then Alexander supposed he had to go back.

And Alexander really hated Azrael and what he was trying to do to the world, so he had to be stopped no matter what.

Alexander smiled to himself. He never wanted to go back but that was the weird thing about being a Witchfinder, it took him all over the world and often to places he really didn't want to go to. He just hadn't expected his home village to be one of those places.

But he was going back with or without the beautiful woman he was falling for.

He loved watching Ithane sit on the edge of the bed, talking and resting her hands on the Emperor's forehead. So clearly the strange words she was saying only a moment ago had worked some magic or something.

"And may the Goddess's blessings be upon you as she takes the poison from your veins and purges it from reality," Ithane said.

Alexander went over to the bed and Maxine joined him. The Emperor was a sickly thin man but he was smiling, laughing and colour was returning to him. His skin returned to a normal colour and his teeth were whitening again.

Alexander couldn't help but stare as the Emperor's black rotting teeth turned healthy. That was amazing and brilliant.

Ithane came over to him. "The Emperor doesn't know it but the Goddess sent him a vision in a dream warning him about the attack. She got him to move to this chamber instead,"

"Is there anything you don't know or can't do?" Alexander asked smiling.

Ithane playfully punched his arm and Alexander laughed, he loved her modesty.

"Your Highness," the Emperor said. "Sorry, Lady Tano,"

Alexander unfolded his arms and smiled as Ithane gracefully went over to him.

"I hereby declare by Royal Decree that everyone in my Empire is to treat you how they would treat me. As a thank you for your service, you hold the power of Regent, Chief Watch and anything else you need in your quest,"

Alexander was shocked. That was a hell of a gift to give Ithane. He wasn't exactly sure where the power he had given her ended, because Ithane could do whatever the hell she wanted in his Empire.

"Thank you your Lordship," Ithane said bowing, "and whilst I am not rude enough to reject such an honour. There is only one blessing I need right now,"

"And you have my Blessing," the Emperor said frowning. "Kill my daughter for what she allowed to happen to my people,"

"Thank you," Alexander said a moment before Ithane could and the Emperor winked at him.

Ithane and Alexander and Maxine bowed and left the bed chamber.

"So," Maxine said, "what now?"

Alexander just looked at Ithane and grinned. "We have to find Jasmine and deal with our original prey,"

"Exactly," Ithane said, "and I have a pretty good idea where to find them,"

CHAPTER 19

I couldn't help but grin as me, Maxine and sexy Alexander rode into the City of Barabara because all the wonderful men, women and children in their perfectly clean clothes and tunics just stopped what they were doing and stared at us. A lot of them were standing on the wooden planks that ran between all the little wooden shacks.

I was so damn happy that the mud was gone and the air no longer smelt of poo. Instead it smelt refreshing with delightful hints of rose, lavender and mint from the fields just outside the City.

The men took the children inside the little wooden shacks because everyone knew what was about to happen, and no one was gesturing that we should stop. No one thought of us as the enemy, I would have sensed it otherwise and I could sense that everyone was excited for why we were here.

For we were here to kill Lady Barabara and Maric who were right in front of us.

I looked down at Lady Barabara, a slim, middle-aged woman wearing the finest red and white and blue silk robes money could buy. She could have used that money to better her people but instead she had wasted it on fine clothing she didn't need.

A solid gold sword swung her waste with more diamonds, sapphires and rubies than I had ever seen before. Again money that could have benefited her people, instead she had wasted it.

Maric was standing next to her and he was frowning. He actually looked shocked to see me, like it was a miracle I had somehow survived what had happened. I quickly searched his mind and he didn't know anything else about Azrael, or nothing useful.

I slid off my horse and Alexander and Maxine flanked me.

"Lady Barabara of the Plotmeny Empire," I said authority filling my voice, "you are a heretic against the people of this world,"

"Impossible," she said laughing.

"You have left your people to suffer, starve and live in hellish conditions whilst you get richer and richer and live a life of greatness at their expense," I said.

I was hating her more and more with each passing second.

"And worse of all," I said, "you conspire with an agent of Azrael to kill your husband, the Emperor, so you can gain more power and influence that would make even more people suffer,"

Lady Barabara grinned.

"For these crimes, there can be no repentance, no forgiveness and no chance for absolution," I said.

I whipped out my sword and I was fairly sure now the Goddess was totally influencing my words and actions. I didn't mind.

I went over to Lady Barabara and Maric actually stood in front of her. I didn't care either way.

I swung my sword.

Lady Barabara screamed and Maric hissed in agony as they were beheaded. Their heads rolled across the floor and their bodies slumped to the ground.

"That wasn't needed," Jasmine shouted as she ran over to me. "They were good people and they were just trying to help me,"

I shook my head and I smiled as Alexender and Maxine grabbed a handful of dirt and threw it over her.

"You might not have killed anyone, you might not have wanted so many people to die and you might have done this to benefit your father," I said, "but everything that has happened in the last two days has happened because of your actions."

"No," Jasmine said.

Maxine stepped forward. "Yes, if you hadn't allowed the Traders Guild to abuse their power then none of this would have happened,"

"Exactly," Alexander said, "and if you hadn't allowed Georgia free rein on this empire then so many would still be alive. Including all the victims of the Guild's traders, slavers and abusers,"

Jasmine shook her head and sank to her knees. "I was just trying to help my father,"

I wanted to help her or forgive her but so many people had died because of her actions and no one liked her, respected her or thought she was going to be a better person. Lady Jasmine had always been an evil person and I was finally going to give her victims justice.

I went over to her and looked her in the eye and she only grinned at me. She didn't feel sorry, she didn't regret this and I doubted she had even done this for her father.

I beheaded her.

A moment later everyone cheered and hugged and kissed each other. Then someone shouted about a party in an hour and everyone rushed inside their wooden shacks.

"What are they doing?" Maxine asked.

"Probably making pies, cakes and getting changed," I said grinning.

I flat out loved being the Goddess's will incarnate and helping wonderful people to change their lives for the better. It was a great feeling, a feeling I was always going to love.

I went back over to my horse. "I take it we're leaving for your home village?"

"Yeah," Alexander said smiling.

I was never going to grow tired of that wonderful, beautiful smile. Alexander was such a perfect man that I was looking forward to spending a lot more time with.

"We have to save it," he said. "We have to protect the innocent that's our job, right?"

I almost frowned and bit my lower lip over the innocent life that had been lost earlier today, but I didn't. Because it was true that the Watchman had been an innocent, but it didn't make me a bad person or a failure. I had still saved lives and as I saw it, if I hadn't had accidently killed him then I would be dead.

And so many other lives would die or suffer if I wasn't there to save them. So I would always honour that Watchman and try to stop other innocent people dying, but sometimes, rarely it was a sad consequence for the greater good.

A sad fact but a true fact.

I nodded. "In the name of the Goddess, we protect the innocent and we have to stop Azrael whoever he is,"

"But it's weird, isn't it?" Maxine asked. "That nothing in the past two days really connects back to Azrael. This entire event happened because the Traders Guild wanted to take over the Plotmeny Empire and they made a bargain with the God,"

I nodded. "So whilst we've been distracted here, what the hell has Azrael been doing?"

Alexender climbed back up on his horse and smiled. "I have a feeling we're about to find out. Care to join me?"

Me and Maxine both laughed at the beautiful man as we climbed up on our horses and we rode off into the night, following our friend and the man I loved because he was a great man and he needed to do this not only for the innocent lives at stake, but for himself too. I didn't know his past but I had a feeling that once we had dealt with the home village crisis.

Then maybe, just maybe a weight would be lifted off Alexender's chest.

And hopefully I would learn more about Azrael.

But that was tomorrow's problem, we had months of travel ahead of us and I fully intended to enjoy the travel, the laughs and meals with my two best friends along the way.

We had done a great job here helping people, defeating evil and giving innocents their freedom back, but there was still a lot of work to do in the future.

And that future was going to be a lot of fun indeed.

AVAILABLE AT ALL MAJOR BOOKSELLERS!

AUTHOR OF THE BETTIE ENGLISH PRIVATE EYE SERIES

CONNOR WHITELEY

EIGHT HOURS

A BETTIE PRIVATE EYE MYSTERY NOVELLA

8 HOURS
A Bettie Private Eye Mystery Novella

CHAPTER 1
18th October 2023
Canterbury, England
7:30

Even the best private eyes get strange cases at times.

Private Eye Bettie English definitely liked the awfully dark morning as autumn had started to set in properly. She sat on her large black sofa with a wonderful piping hot mug of bitter black coffee in her hand and she was so looking forward to today.

She had the large black TV on in the background but she had muted it because the news was just talking about a bunch of political scandals that were just getting old by now.

Bettie liked the darkness outside and she had the bright white crystal lights on and Bettie had to admit they were certainly the best things she had ever bought herself. The crystals looked so classy, expensive and they really did light up the place.

And the cream walls of the living gave room off the glow perfectly, but Bettie really did miss the summer because at least when she got up it wasn't pitch black outside.

Exactly like it was now.

She had given herself the day off of being the President of The British Private Eye Federation so she could thankfully spend the entire day with her two beautiful children Elizabeth and Harrison, before her boyfriend Detective Graham Adams came home later today.

Bettie was so excited about seeing and spending the whole day with her kids on a weekday. She had never imagined she would be like that but she loved her kids, loved her family and life was just brilliant.

The sweet aromas of pancakes, chocolate syrup and caramel sauce filled the air as bangs, sizzling and popping came out of the kitchen. Bettie smiled to herself as her amazing nephew Sean and his boyfriend Harry were cooking up breakfast for everyone.

She loved having them live with them. Bettie supposed it might have been because Sean's mother kicked him and Harry out after the homophobic attack in June 2022 that left Harry with a brain injury. But now they were both recovered Bettie just loved having them here.

Especially when they cooked breakfast for everyone.

"Breakfast's almost ready Auntie," Sean said from the kitchen.

"Thanks," Bettie said.

She was almost tempted to go and wake up the kids but this was the first time in ages they had slept after six am. She had checked on them and they were just snoring away so they were okay and Bettie just fully intended to relax and just enjoy the peace and quiet.

The news on the TV flashed a little as some breaking news came in, Bettie rolled her eyes and unmuted it. She might have well heard about it in case it was important.

A very tall blond woman with a dangerously thin body appeared on the TV. Bettie hated models and reporters being that thin, it did nothing to help women and their body image.

"Breaking news today from the Home Office. The UK Government and Kent Police has confirmed this is the final day for the search of Canterbury Lake in hope of finding evidence that the murdered 18-year-old girl, Sarah Hill was killed here,"

Bettie nodded. She had no idea the police were searching a lake in connection with a murder, but she had been busy up in London for the past few weeks trying to figure out how to convince more people to become private eyes and boost membership in the process.

"Here you go Auntie," Sean said walking in a piping hot plate with two waffles on it with whipped cream, chocolate syrup and caramel sauce on top.

The perfect breakfast for private eyes.

Bettie smiled at Sean and Harry as they both bought in their own breakfasts in their matching white t-shirt, black jogging bottoms and socks like they normally did when they didn't have to go to the university to help out doing some research.

Bettie admired Sean's tasteful pink highlights in his longish blond hair for a moment before she just couldn't help but ask about this case on the news.

"You two have friends down near Canterbury Lake, don't you?" Bettie asked.

Sean nodded. "Yeah and we went to a party there at the weekend. It's massive and the cops have been swarming the lake for days,"

Bettie was really tempted to call Graham to see what he knew because as she wanted to spend the day with the kids, she would have normally loved a nice big juicy case to sink her teeth into. It would have been amazing fun.

"You want to investigate?" Harry asked.

Bettie grinned. "It would be fun and come on, a murdered young woman possibly dumped in a lake. Wouldn't that be interesting?"

"What would dad say?" Sean asked.

It took Bettie a few moments to realise that he was talking about Graham. She was still getting used to him calling Graham dad and not uncle or just Graham. She knew that Sean and Harry were basically family and Sean was legally her son but it was still taking some getting used to.

Bettie was about to continue when someone knocked at the door and Bettie just huffed. All she wanted to do was simply eat her pancakes.

Bettie got up, went over to the front door and she was surprised to see a very short woman in a business suit standing there and Graham was behind her.

This couldn't be good. Bettie had no idea why Graham would come home so early.

Bettie opened the door and she smiled at Graham but he frowned at her.

The woman extended her hand. "Miss English, my name is Isabella Hill and we need you to solve the murder of my daughter by 4 pm today,"

"Otherwise," Graham said, "a rapist and murder walks free forever,"

And Bettie just grinned because that was exactly the sort of case that she wanted.

CHAPTER 2
18th October 2023
Canterbury, England
7:45

Detective Graham Adams really did enjoy the darkness of the autumn mornings because they were just so mysterious, dark and they suggested that anything could happen. And for the briefest of moments, he almost believed that he wasn't just going to be spending the entire day doing paperwork for lazy-ass detectives that wanted to punish him for being incorruptible and a hard-ass.

Graham hugged Harrison as him and Elizabeth had just awoken up and he wanted hugs with his dad. Graham never ever had a problem with that, so he sat on the black sofa as Sean fixed him and Isabella a plate of waffles each.

Graham knew he had to be careful to make sure Harrison The Vulture didn't steal all of his food, but he was just so cute that he knew it was going to happen. Just like how he knew that Elizabeth was going to steal all of Bettie's food.

Damn, he loved his kids.

Graham had to admit that Isabella was wearing a very fitting business suit that definitely highlighted her fit, gym body, thin legs and arms and she just looked good. She was nothing compared to Bettie but he could understand why Mr Hill had loved her.

"So what's this all about?" Bettie asked him.

Graham smiled. He did love being a floater detective so he wasn't tied down to any single department in Kent Police but his job certainly made explaining things hard at times.

"You must be aware that the police are searching Canterbury Lake for evidence," Graham said.

"Sort of but what's the case?" Bettie asked.

Isabella sliced into her waffles. "Two years ago my beautiful daughter Sarah was going to a club and after party at some uni friend's house. She never made it home that night or any night since,"

"God," Bettie said giving Elizabeth some waffle.

"Daddy?" Harrison asked.

Harrison just looked at Graham like that was so unfair. Graham laughed and gave his precious angel a piece.

"The police searched for a week they didn't find her. They conducted a murder investigation after they found a knife covered in dried blood in the house of the party but it later turned out the blood was fake. No one knows what happened to the daughter," Graham said.

Bettie nodded. "Okay, I presume the case went cold so what's happening with the Lake?"

"Now that is definitely where things get interesting." Graham said smiling. "Two weeks ago a dying man in a German prison contacted the British Embassy after saying that he spent time in a cell with an English man claiming to have raped, killed and buried three young women in a lake in Canterbury,"

Isabella took a mouthful of her waffle. Graham did the same, he couldn't believe the sensational explosion of fluffiness and flavour in his mouth, it was amazing.

"So what happened next?" Sean asked.

"The British Ambassador reported this to the Foreign Office who passed it onto the Home Office who passed it onto the police and after three hours of receiving the information the police launched the search," Graham said.

"Mummy?" Elizabeth asked.

Bettie laughed as she gave her daughter another piece of waffle and before Harrison could ever react Graham passed him another piece.

"Love you daddy,"

Graham just laughed.

"Do you know what made the police act so quickly?" Bettie asked.

"The offender," Graham asked.

"The monster and rapist you mean," Isabella said.

"It turned out that Alex White was spotted and interviewed by police as part of the original investigation and since that time he has been arrested on suspicions of rape three separate times in three separate cities but the women later cantered their statements before one of their family members always had a strange fall down the stairs," Graham said.

Graham absolutely hated talking about this monster but it was why he had come to Bettie because if anyone could put this monster away forever it would be her.

"Okay," Harry said, "so the police believe they have a lead but why the lake and most importantly why did you mention a deadline?"

Isabella frowned. "The police say they are looking for the bodies of the three young women and they don't know where they are exactly. They are just in the lake somewhere,"

Graham nodded. "And the deadline is because Alex White has booked a one-way ticket to the USA that is taking off at 4 pm. There is no evidence so we cannot charge him or arrest him and we both know that extradition once he gets to the USA will be difficult,"

"Giving him another chance to flee," Bettie said.

Bettie finished off her waffles and smiled. "So we have eight hours to solve a murder, find evidence and stop a killer from escaping forever,"

"Not a short order then," Graham said grinning.

"If in case we do take the case," Bettie said, "and we find the worse. Are there are any marks on her body that we can use to identify her?"

Isabella frowned. "Not really but she does have fractures on her left arm from a boating accident she had four years ago. Is that helpful?"

Graham had no idea but Bettie seemed pleased.

"Will you all help me?" Isabella said.

Graham, Sean and Harry just looked at Bettie, their fearless leader and they all grinned as she nodded.

"Let's get the bastard,"

CHAPTER 3
18th October 2023
Canterbury, England
08:00

Alex White leant against the cold white wall of his small expensive hotel room as he got out his phone and bought up the news coverage of the police digging and searching and investigating the lake where his victims were meant to be.

He enjoyed the icy coldness of the walls and he almost wondered for a moment if this was the same icy coldness that his victims felt before he killed them. Maybe they did but he didn't care, he had chosen this expensive little hotel because it was quick, easy and it would give him a good night of sleep before he fled forever.

The English cops were never ever going to be as brilliant as him so he wasn't scared about the police finding the victims. That was pointless, and even if the police did find them then their backlog and rules and regulations would slow them down too much.

He would be able to leave at 4 pm and then he would be free to fly over to the USA.

The US always had such pretty little women just walking about in their short-shorts and bras.

Alex was so looking forward to hunting them down, stalking them and then killing them again. It wouldn't even be much of a challenge for him to fool the American doughnut-eating cops.

He would escape, the pattern would continue and then Alex would finally be free of law enforcement to kill whatever woman he wanted.

No one was smart enough to stop him and that made him far happier than he ever wanted to admit.

CHAPTER 4
18th October 2023
Canterbury, England
8:20

Bettie was so damn happy to finally have a juicy, amazing case that she could really sink her teeth into, instead of the nightmare paperwork she had been doing for the Federation for weeks.

It might have taken them a little longer to set up the three massive whiteboards in the living room, but Bettie didn't mind. It was finally done and she could finally start to investigate the case properly.

The very last thing she wanted to do was just trust the police had done their job properly the first time only to realise hours later that they hadn't done it well at all.

Bettie having little Harrison and Elizabeth walk around her feet as they had streaks of chocolate and caramel sauce on their faces as they had secretly grabbed her plate when she wasn't looking.

Sean and Harry were trying to gently grab them so they could wipe their mouth and Bettie really did love her family of wonderful chaos.

At least the bright blue sky was starting to show now and Bettie had to admit the outside wasn't as dark, depressing and scary as earlier. But now all that Bettie wanted to do was investigate this awful crime and just make sure Alex White died in prison.

"Everyone ready," Graham said.

Bettie nodded and she folded her arms as she looked at the whiteboards that were covered in a few crime scene photos, a few lab reports and just a general timeline about what had happened.

"We're here,"

Bettie looked down at her black laptop and grinned as she saw her two best friends in the entire world on the screen. Senior Forensic Specialist Zoey Quill was in her long white lab coat like she always was and Bettie could see her assistant Fran was in the back of an SUV, probably driving down from London to help them.

"Let's start at the beginning," Bettie said. "We know that on the 31st of October 2021 Sarah Hill went to a Halloween party at a friend's house at university,"

"It's the same party every year," Sean said, "and 2021, me and Harry would have been there. Want to hear how the party went?"

Bettie nodded. It would be amazing to have some lived experience about the party.

"The party was in the same massive masonry mansion that it's always in. There's music, a ton of alcohol and because it is university there are always drugs going round. And no, me and Harry never do drugs,"

"My daughter didn't either," Isabella said.

Bettie weakly smiled at her. Maybe she should have sent Isabella home, but if something had happened to Harrison or Elizabeth she would have wanted to know too.

"The party was great. There was no drama, no fights and compare to the Halloween party last year, it was silent. Everyone was in costume and then everyone uses the bedroom for adult activities,"

"Did you?" Graham asked grinning.

Sean shrugged. "I honestly can't remember. Too much alcohol past midnight,"

Bettie smiled. It was good to know there weren't any fights or anything that dramatic that happened at the party and it did explain why the police reports were so thin on details. There was simply nothing to report.

"Let's go back to the case files," Bettie said.

"We know Sarah arrived at the party with her three best friends at 9 pm and the last reported sighting of Sarah was at midnight when she was seen going upstairs alone with a drink in her hand," Graham said.

"Then what?" Bettie asked going towards the whiteboards.

"Unknown, there is no forensic evidence, no sightings, not even camera footage of anyone seeing her," Graham said.

"What?" Fran asked. "A bunch of university students taking photos and everyone don't take a photo of a missing girl,"

Bettie had to agree. It was strange that out of the hundred-plus university students there that basically lived on their phones and not a single person had taken a photo of her. Especially with the party not finishing until 3 am.

That just didn't happen in this day and age.

Bettie went over to a whiteboard and pointed to the theory of the lead investigator.

"He supposed," Bettie said, "that Sarah simply went upstairs and came back down without anyone noticing,"

"Not exactly a lot of focus," Harry said holding his head.

Bettie frowned a little. She knew talking about the police was always a dodgy topic to talk about with Harry considering it was a police officer that had given Harry his brain injury that he was thankfully recovered from.

"What about the forensics?" Bettie asked. "Anything you believe can be relooked at?"

Zoey sighed. "I doubt it. A lot has changed in forensics within the past two years and without a body or something to go on my hands and powers are limited,"

"Okay thanks anyway,"

"I hope you find anything. Contact me again if you find some evidence," Zoey said looking about as sad and annoyed as Bettie felt.

She knew there was a missing girl that was probably dead here but she just had no idea how to find the evidence and the body.

No idea at all.

CHAPTER 5
18th October 2023
Canterbury, England
8:40

Graham was absolutely shocked that out of the hundreds upon hundreds of university students actually at the party that night, not a single person had taken a picture of Sarah Hill after midnight. That made no sense and even he took endless photos whenever he was out and about.

Graham stood right next to sexy Bettie as they both stared at the massive whiteboards just hoping to spot something else before they moved onto the next part of the case. He couldn't even begin to imagine what poor Isabella was going through but that was why he just had to get the bastard behind all of this.

He had to find out what had happened to Sarah Hill two years ago and he was really hoping to find out what had happened to the other two women that were meant to be buried at the lake.

"Nothing," Fran said. "I've reran all the social media footage and pictures through our

AI programme and there was no more photos after midnight of Sarah Hill,"

Graham was glad that Fran had double-checked that but right now it was flat out bizarre. Sarah Hill had to get out of that house somehow without anyone seeing her and that just seemed impossible.

"How did the police search the mansion?" Bettie asked.

Graham went over to the whiteboard and Elizabeth almost ran into his leg but Sean grabbed her before she could.

Graham looked at the police report. "Twenty officers searched the mansion top to bottom using dogs too. They searched each room twice over the course of a day and they found nothing,"

"Since when are the police that thorough?" Sean asked.

Graham couldn't disagree.

Isabella laughed. "Let's say when you have a small fortune left over from your husband's death and you give a chunk of it to the police, that is a great incentive,"

Graham shrugged. It wasn't a bad reason, he just wished the police didn't have to be effectively bought at times but budget cuts were budget cuts.

Bettie placed her hands on her sexy hips. "What about after midnight? You haven't mentioned what happened then?"

Graham had only seen the case two hours ago he hadn't read all of it yet but Sean and Harry were already bringing up something on their laptops.

"Kent Police conducted a search of the mansion and the surrounding property for two days and they didn't find anything." Sean said. "Or they admit they did but because of the party atmosphere they had no idea what should and shouldn't have been there,"

Graham rolled his eyes. It wasn't bad police work but he had been to a lot of crime scenes over the years like that, and it was damn well annoying as hell when that happened.

It annoyed him more than life itself. Why on earth couldn't criminals just pick a nice clean crime scene to do their offenses on?

Graham went over to the whiteboards and double-checked a small list of things the police officers wanted to highlight in their case notes but refused to add to the official file because it wasn't strong enough evidence.

There were a few drag marks but they equally could have been marks were someone had fallen over whilst drunk.

They had nothing.

"Daddy," Elizabeth said holding a small orange ball that Graham took from her and dropped it on her head so she laughed and ran away chasing after it.

"Let's say," Bettie said, "that she or her…"

"You can say it," Isabella said.

Graham could see how badly she didn't want to say it.

"Her killer," Bettie said, "managed to find a way out of the mansion. Then what? Presumably Alex White would want to interfere with her and then kill her?"

"What about here?" Fran said on the laptop.

Graham nodded as he watched Fran bring up a large map of the local area in the middle of a forest and tons of empty fields.

"The killer could have taken her anywhere," Graham said.

Bettie shook her head. "No, a dead body

is easy to carry but still. You wouldn't want to be carrying a dead body over anything too extreme or hilly,"

"Is that why I've never seen any of your exes?" Graham asked asking smiling.

Bettie shrugged. "Keeping asking questions like that and you might find out and I'll find out how easy your body is to carry,"

Graham just laughed but he still couldn't deny that they were no closer now than they had been an hour ago in finding out exactly what had happened to Sarah Hill.

They had to turn their attention to how exactly Alex White had turned into a suspect and then Graham knew they were going to have to visit the lake.

And hopefully find her body.

CHAPTER 6
18th October 2023
Canterbury, England
9:05

Bettie really wasn't impressed with how good the original police work on the case was, they seemed to have done all the logical things, processed everything correctly and they had had a lot of good instincts. But they had all proven themselves wrong.

Bettie normally liked bad police work because it was so much easier to solve and see where the police had gone wrong, but for a change they simply hadn't made a mistake. Which was unique for the police but there was a first time for everything.

Bettie hugged Harrison tight as she looked at Fran and Sean who were looking through the police files about how Alex White had first been dismissed as a suspect and then later reappeared as the prime suspect.

"Here," Sean said. "Alex White was interviewed at 10 am the day after the party but the police didn't suspect anything was wrong at the time so they only asked the basic questions,"

Bettie really didn't like that the police might have made a mistake that early on in the investigation.

"The police asked him," Sean said, "questions like did he see anything odd at the party, did he see Sarah and stuff like that,"

"Where you two questioned?" Bettie asked.

Harry smiled. "No, we were contacted and they emailed us in the university accommodation but we had massive hangovers and…"

Bettie couldn't understand why Harry had just stopped and looked at Sean.

Sean clicked his fingers. "And it wasn't compulsory. Graham, how many people at the party did the police actually interview and did they ever find out the exact number of people at the party?"

Bettie smiled. She couldn't believe the police hadn't tried to track down every single person. Granted it would have been impossible with their limited resources and budgets but they still might have learnt something about Sarah's death, or at that point disappearance.

"They interviewed twenty people and the students that hired the mansion had no idea how many came that night. At least 120 people,"

Bettie laughed and kissed Harrison on the cheek as he laughed too. The police hadn't even tried to contact more than a third of the guests at the party.

"That means someone might have seen her without taking a photo and just didn't realise it," Bettie said. "Let's turn back to Alex White,"

Fran nodded on the laptop and the loud rushing of air behind her made Bettie really hopeful that she was almost in Canterbury. It would be great to see her.

"He graduated from Kent University that summer, went to different cities, got involved in different rape accusations and nothing ever stuck,"

Bettie hated this sick bastard.

"He always claimed that women got jealous when he turned them down," Fran said.

Now Bettie really, really wanted to punch him.

Sean clicked his fingers and everyone went over to look at his laptop and Bettie just grinned.

"Here," Sean said. "Kent Police confirmed using mobile phone location data that Alex White was in the area of the lake at the time of the party and the day after. A wild life camera confirms seeing Alex throwing something very large into the lake,"

"Have you got the image babe?" Harry asked kissing Sean on the cheek.

Bettie was surprised when Sean bought up the image and it was crystal clear. She couldn't believe she was watching Alex, a very tall, thin, athletic-looking man throwing a large black bag or some sort into the lake,"

"Wait," Bettie said looking back at the muted TV that still had the news on. "If the image told the police to look there why are they setting up camp somewhere else?"

Everyone looked at Bettie and she had no idea what to tell them. The fact was the picture showed Alex throwing the bag into the lake near some oak trees but the police according to the news were cornering off a very large sandy area of the lake on the opposite side.

It made no sense at all.

And Bettie couldn't understand what the police knew that she didn't. The Federation had access to a whole bunch of private, police and international databases.

Everything the police knew Bettie should have had access to.

"So what's happened in the past few hours or day that's made their way into the command centre but not the computer systems?" Bettie asked.

"We need to find out. Now," Graham said.

Bettie couldn't agree more.

CHAPTER 7
18th October 2023
Canterbury, England
10:30

After all the awful Canterbury traffic, after all the awful news reporters that created a brilliant human wall to slow them down and after negotiating with the police that they were allowed onto the lake site, Graham was so damn pleased to finally be standing right outside the massive white canvas tent forming the police command centre.

Graham leant on the icy cold Federation-issue SUV next to the woman he loved as he dug his feet into the even colder sand and just waited for the Police Commander to come and talk to them.

Graham had no idea what he was going to tell him but he needed to make sure the

Commander allowed them to investigate on-site. And as much as it had killed him to drop off Isabella at home because she really wanted to be apart of this, he knew it was the right thing to do.

It had been bad enough having to handover Harrison and Elizabeth to Bettie's mum for the rest of the day. Even though the kids hardly cared they were going to have a great day whoever had them.

Graham really missed them both. He loved them so damn much.

The immense, thick oak trees that lined the edge of the even larger lake blew gently in the icy cold wind and the whacking of branches made Graham almost jump the first few times.

The rich smell of rot, coffee and bacon sandwiches filled the air as Graham realised the police were dredging the banks of the lake and he really didn't want to know why.

There were large crowds of white-suited crime scene techs around them searching the sand, the sand bars and the water with long metal poles for any sign or evidence of what had happened to poor Sarah Hill and the other two victims that they were meant to be buried here.

Graham couldn't imagine the sheer terror, agony and desperation the women would have been in when Alex White had taken them here to rape and kill them. If he wasn't such a rule follower he might have killed the monster himself, but that was a crime.

Graham never committed a crime, or at least a serious one in the name of justice.

"Detective Adams," a short man said wearing full-on police uniform like he was about to be on parade or something.

"Commander," Graham said shaking the man's hand. "This is my nephew Sean English, his boyfriend Harry and my wonderful girlfriend,"

The Commander folded his arms. "President Bettie English I never thought I would have the so-called honour. I appreciate what you do but this is a real crime scene,"

Fran stepped forward. "I'm Fran, I am Bettie's Assistant Commander Knight,"

Graham was impressed she had already researched him.

"It doesn't matter who you are," Knight said. "This is my investigation, my crime scene and my search operation and we only have less than six hours,"

"Then," Bettie said," I suggest you allow us to help because we have access to technology the police cannot afford,"

Knight laughed. "This is why the police have gone to pot. All you youngsters want to do is use technology instead of good old fashion police work,"

Graham couldn't believe the idiot was actually saying this. He was such a nob.

"Have you made any progress in the past two days of searching?" Graham asked knowing that they hadn't.

"We have found a plethora of strange items including needles, condoms and-"

Graham waved him silent. "You found evidence of kids using drugs and having sex at the lake. Big deal and you know it. You need to find evidence of corpses here and we can help,"

Sean nodded as Harry stepped forward. "Me and Sean do Advanced Technological Engineering at university. We have the drones and can create-"

Knight placed a firm hand over Harry's

mouth and Graham had to force himself not to charge or something. No one touched his family but then he realised he might be overreacting because of Bettie's assassination attempt two months ago.

He didn't dare tell her but some nights he woke up sweating because of it.

"I don't care about your so-called fancy technology. I will give you ten minutes to get off my crime scene or I will arrest you and damn the consequences," Knight said as he walked away.

Graham just smiled at the sexy woman he loved as he was fairly sure Knight had no idea what the consequences were of going up against the Federation, considering the organisation had more power than some small countries.

"We have to get on that lake," Bettie said. "We could call the Police commissioner but I want other ideas first,"

Graham smiled at Sean and Harry. "I have an idea but it's risky. Can you fly over the lake and run a scan or something as you're flying and transmit it back to your computer in case it's destroyed?"

Graham laughed as Sean's eyes widened and Harry hugged him tight. Clearly Sean hated the idea of innocent drones being shot down but he knew it was starting to become standard police procedure to some extent.

He doubted Knight wouldn't order a drone to be taken down.

"I could," Sean said, "but the fact remains the data won't be good,"

"We'll have one shot to scan a small area," Harry said.

Graham hugged Bettie. "Then we scan the area where Alex threw the black bag into the lake,"

CHAPTER 8
18th October 2023
Canterbury, England
11:00

Bettie couldn't believe how much of a total nob and dickhead that stupid Commander Knight was. It was clear the police needed all the help they could get and because of Knight's stupidity a sexual predator and murder was going to walk away free.

Yet again.

Bettie leant against the icy cold bark of an oak tree at the very edge of the lake looking out at Sean and Harry as they finished setting up the drone. It was a very small commercial thing that Bettie hated to know how much the cameras, frame and more high-tech stuff had cost them.

It wasn't cheap.

Bettie was glad Graham and Fran were parked on the dirt road next to the wire fence they had cut to get access to the lake. It was technically trespassing but when a sex offender was on the loose, Bettie really didn't care about stupid rules and laws.

Bettie crouched down next to the lovers and she couldn't deny Harry smelt great today with his rich earthy aftershave that Sean had bought him for his birthday a few months back.

Sean was connecting his laptop to the drone and Bettie was really impressed how well and quickly they were working to get the drone operational.

"Here," Harry said.

There was a green flashing light on the

massive remote control he was holding so Bettie guessed that the drone was connected and a moment later Bettie's face appeared on Sean's laptop.

Bettie looked out over the swirling, twirling and whirling cold water of the lake that almost looked as black as night but it was the three police speedboats out on the water that concerned her.

She hadn't seen the speedboats earlier so they were new, and she didn't want to take a chance of them getting caught because as soon as the drone was launched their location would be revealed.

"Sean," Bettie said really not wanting to say what she was going to say. "Is there any chance you can go off deeper into the woods please?"

"You think we're going to get caught," Sean said.

"Exactly," Bettie said, "and when we do I would rather not have you and your laptop taken away. I would rather you hold up somewhere, analyse the footage and have something for us when we get out,"

Harry smiled and rolled his eyes. "And I'm the expendable one,"

Bettie knew he was joking so she nodded. "Very much so,"

Sean kissed Harry and Bettie goodbye and then she watched him run off into the woods. His laptop held firmly by his chest.

"I can launch and start running the scan whenever," Harry said.

Bettie was glad about that but she was concentrating on the police boats now. They all seemed to be coming towards them slowly, almost like they didn't want to be noticed by her.

They were clearly failing but Bettie had no idea if there were secret cameras, wildlife cameras or anything else that would have alerted the police to their movements.

A camera had probably taken a photo or two and now Knight wanted to arrest them. The dumb idiot.

"Launch," Bettie said knowing they were out of time.

Harry nodded and the drone silently came alive and zoomed over the surface of the water.

The police boats flared to life.

"Get that scan done," Bettie said.

Harry didn't react.

Bettie watched the drone zoom over the surface of the water and she just hoped beyond hope that the drone was sending Sean high-definition scans of the lakebed.

A police boat smashed into the drone.

Making it fall into the water.

Harry grinned so Bettie guessed the drone was still scanning and transmitting for a little while at least.

Bettie smiled as the police boats zoomed towards the shore and she was half tempted to run away but it was useless. She knew that Graham and Fran were already in custody and they were just waiting for her.

It was all just a big waste of time because it wouldn't take too long for her lawyer to turn up to sort out everything. And if that failed Bettie would just call the UK government and with a little blackmail she would be released.

As the police boats gently glided into the shore and three black uniformed police officers stormed towards them, Bettie really shook her head at this utter waste of time.

If the police had just allowed her to investigate they would easily find the evidence to put Alex White away forever.

As two strong, muscular hands gripped Bettie's shoulders she really felt sorry for all of Alex White's past, present and future victims.

Then the police took her away.

CHAPTER 9
18th October 2023
Canterbury, England
12:30

Graham was seriously fuming as he sat on the damn cold wooden bench at the edge of the white-canvas tent of the police command centre. It was just so damn stupid that Knight had arrested him and Graham had given up for an hour ago trying to free himself from the stupid handcuffs.

Of course sexy Bettie had slipped out of her handcuffs more times than he cared to think, but that was why she was amazing and he loved her more than anything else in the world.

Graham watched as tons of police officers in their thick black coats sat around looking at large laptop screens as voices came from the radio, everyone was relaying information and now the divers were finally exploring the lake.

The awful smell of burnt coffee, charred bacon and damp filled the air and Graham couldn't understand what was taking Bettie's lawyer so bloody long to get here.

Knight smiled at Graham as he took a phone call and leant on a massive white plastic table covering the middle of the command centre.

Graham wanted to be investigating, helping, just doing something instead of sitting here.

"I'm sorry," Bettie said just playing with her handcuffs like they were mere toys in her hands.

"What for?" Graham asked.

"For coming up with the idea that got you arrested," she said.

Graham looked at Fran and Harry who had managed to get one hand out of their handcuffs but were struggling to get the other one out, not that it really mattered.

"When Phryne coming?" Graham asked, knowing Bettie would have called her sister of all people to come and be their lawyer.

A loud crackling sound came over the radio.

Knight grabbed a walkie-talkie.

"Commander we have it. We have it. We have discovered three black plastic boxes large enough for corpses," a woman said.

"Bring them up," Knight said and then he turned to Bettie. "See we didn't need any Private Eye rubbish,"

Graham shook his head as Knight walked away. He was such an idiot and he really doubted that Alex White would have been so silly and used plastic boxes.

"He's too careful for that," Graham said.

"Agreed," Bettie said. "Plastic boxes, I guess like the garden storage ones, the plastic's too thin to withstand the pressure of deep lake water,"

Harry leant forward. "And plastic boxes like that can be airtight, they would float too easily unless he seriously weighted them down,"

Graham hadn't even considered that idea. That actually made it even less likely the corpses were actually in the boxes because he really doubted Alex would have pulled extremely heavy boxes through the surrounding woods and out into the lake.

The bodies weren't in those boxes so the police were chasing their tails yet again.

"We need to get out of here," Graham said.

A very tall woman stormed over. Graham knew she must be the second-in-command or something.

"You are not going anywhere," she said. "I am in charge around here and-"

"Do you want a rapist and killer to escape?" Graham asked. "I am a detective and I will investigate this as I see fit,"

The woman laughed. "And I am a Detective Inspector, I'm only away from my desk because the Top Brass doesn't want idiots like you screwing this up,"

Graham frowned. He hated dealing with police politics and the so-called Top Brass that couldn't know how to investigate a crime even if their lives depended on it.

Bettie gently touched the woman's arm. "Please DI, you know how good I am and you know that I solve cases like no tomorrow. Let us go and-"

"Bettie English I am arresting you for obstructing a police investigation you do not have to say anything but-"

"But nothing," Phryne said as she stormed in.

Graham just nodded his hello to Bettie's sister as she stormed over to the DI wearing a very professional-looking business suit, and Graham wasn't sure if she was going to whack the DI over the head. She looked so angry.

"I am Miss English's legal counsel and I demand you release her,"

The DI laughed as her walkie-talkie buzzed. It was Knight.

"The boxes are empty. They were weight down with cement but the boxes collapsed as soon as the divers tried to move them,"

Graham just looked at the DI, dead in the eye.

"You will free us and you will let us investigate," Graham said firmly.

The DI shook her head. "Negative and Detective Adams, please hand over your badge. I will allow you to leave and you can investigate off-site but if I see you near the Lake again then I will arrest you,"

Graham really hated this stupid woman.

"And you are now on suspension depending on a full investigation into your conduct Detective Adams. You know police rules and regulations and yet you continue to disregard them,"

Graham so badly wanted to spit at the DI's feet but he forced himself not to, so he simply gave the woman his police ID and walked away.

They were now free but because of the police's stupidity they were now seriously running out of time to find the missing bodies and find the evidence that would finally put Alex White away forever.

And Graham hated that.

CHAPTER 10
18th October 2023
Canterbury, England
12:45

Bettie was so damn angry with the stupid police with all their pathetic rules, regulations and she just couldn't believe the police had suspended Graham. She felt guilty as hell because it was her decisions that had led to all of this.

She had to find a way to make it right but even she knew the limits of the Federation's power, influence and favours. When it came to individual police conduct, there wasn't much she could do.

Damn this all to hell.

Bettie hugged Sean tight as the four of them reached the black Federation SUV that was parked on the very edge of the lake's property lines. It was a shame that Phryne said she had to go back to actual lawyer work but she really wanted to see Bettie and Sean again soon.

Bettie had to admit she was starting to love her sister more and more after their recent troubles.

The cold wind howled and blew past the massive oak trees that covered the area, and the huge long dirty road went on for miles before actually hitting civilisation. Maybe that was the key to everything and Bettie couldn't believe she hadn't thought about it sooner.

The police had to know something that they didn't, that was fair enough, but the police also had to have access to the security cameras that lined the single road that led towards the lake with its little offshoots heading into the woodlands and the lake itself.

"Sean," Bettie said knowing she was about to dismiss him almost. "Sorry but I'll ask about the drone scans in a moment. Right now I need to know what the police have seen in this road footage,"

Sean smiled as he searched the police footage on their databases. Bettie could see the police had run the footage through their databases so their tech experts could scan the footage instead of the detectives having to do it.

"Nothing," Sean said. "In the days before and after the murder there are no vehicles coming along this road until the police turn up,"

Bettie nodded. "I don't doubt you but then, how did Alex get onto the property to dump the black bags?"

Sean laughed and he showed Harry something on his laptop.

"Wow," Harry said. "He never did dump the bags here. The photo was faked using Artificial Intelligence,"

Bettie clicked her fingers. That was now really interesting because the single piece of evidence that tied Alex White to the lake was fake and that meant the police were probably looking in the wrong place for the bodies.

Yet Bettie couldn't understand if that was true, then why was Alex running and preparing to leave the UK now? Sure, he could have just decided to leave for the fun of it but she had spoken to sexual predators before like Alex, they were too careful, too cunning, too evil to *just* do something.

There was always a reason.

"Bring up all news footage covering this search," Bettie said.

Fran took out her phone and she was probably doing the same thing. Bettie looked down the long road back towards the lake.

Even the police seemed to be using drones over the lake now, they were always going to be inferior to Sean's but at least they were trying.

"What you looking for?" Graham asked kissing her softly on the neck.

Bettie forced herself not to moan in

pleasure, she loved him but this wasn't the time. Even his touch made her anger and guilt build up and up.

"I want to know what Alex might know about the search,"

"What about the police searching a mile North of the lake originally?" Harry asked showing Bettie his phone.

That would make perfect sense and Bettie supposed that if Alex believed the cops were searching north of the Lake and there was a chance the police were getting too close to the truth then he might naturally want to run.

This wasn't about the lake.

This was all about whatever was a mile north of this awful place.

"I think the scans might be useful now," Sean said frowning.

Bettie couldn't tell if he was annoyed or not for not being able to share too soon.

"I ran topographical analysis, current analysis, weather, wildlife and more analysis than I care to admit but this lake is useless at hiding things. Because if someone threw something in the lake it would travel further, so I know these black bags aren't in there. But I am also saying that there is nothing in the lake at all,"

"Alex White was never here," Bettie said.

"Exactly," Sean said. "Those plastic boxes I did find on the scanning equipment but they were at least three years old judging by my analysis,"

Bettie hugged him as a thanks but that meant the police and everyone had been looking in the wrong place. It was clear that Knight wouldn't want to hear from them but that didn't matter.

They now had a lead.

And Bettie just hoped the delay wouldn't make them lose their chance to catch Alex White before the bastard flew away forever.

CHAPTER 11
18th October 2023
Canterbury, England
13:05

Graham's stomach tightened into a painful knot as he stepped out of the SUV and onto the soft, cold ground of the woodland around them. Immensely tall oaks shot up into the sky like arrows and Graham really had a bad feeling about this.

The woodland ground was covered in leaves, fallen branches and fungi. Graham was almost tempted to get out the fungi and foraging app on his phone but he knew this wasn't the time.

Maybe later, maybe not.

Graham followed as Bettie led them away from the SUV and towards the spot where the police had originally been searching. The loud hum of drones flying about made Graham smile as he watched Harry and Sean control them.

The woodland smelt rich of nature, damp and icy coldness as the air tried to invade his lungs. The air was so cold but he didn't care. He was here for the victims, not to make himself feel warm.

After a few moments, Bettie stopped in the middle of a large circular cleaning. Graham brushed away some of the endless dead leaves on the ground with his foot but that only revealed it was frozen solid.

That was good sign.

"At least if the soil is frozen now,"

Graham said, "that it's likely it was frozen the day after the murders so the bodies couldn't be buried,"

"Excellent point," Bettie said looking up at the trees.

Graham did the same and the huge branches of the oaks shooting out in all directions were wonderful to look at and they showed just how impressive nature could be. But there was something off about them.

He couldn't exactly place his finger on it but as the cold wind brushed his cheeks, he realised something really was off.

Graham went into the centre of the clearing and noticed the oak branches seemed to just stop after they got so far into the clearing.

Then he looked at the other trees and their trunks and he realised that the trunks were covered in silver lichens, probably caused by the pollution the cold wind constantly brought down from the motorway less than a mile away. But none of the branches had lichens on.

He knew from his biology classes at school that lichens provided protection for trees so if they were taken away then the branches were weakened.

Causing them to stop over time.

Graham frowned as he couldn't believe that little detail wasn't going to help them on the case. It was just a weird little quirk of nature.

"Can you scan the area please?" Graham asked.

Harry shook his head. "The soil's too hard to get good readings from. We can get a few centimetres below the surface but that's it,"

Bettie sighed. "We need to focus and let's think like Alex,"

"I would rather not," Fran said.

Graham couldn't disagree.

"We've just killed a young woman that's barely 18, we've done some stuff to her and killed her. Why this location?"

Graham took out his phone and checked the distance between here and the mansion.

"Mansion's only one mile East," Graham said. "Not a bad place to dump a body because I doubt a lot of university students, very drunk ones, would travel this far through steep woodland to follow Alex,"

Sean laughed. "Believe me no drunk student would make it through these woods,"

Graham was about to say something but he frowned. "Not a single drunk student. Would that mean Alex would have to carry a drunk woman through the woodland with him,"

"With Sarah constantly moving like drunk people do," Bettie said.

Fran shook her head. "Could it be done?"

Graham picked up Bettie and threw her over his shoulder. Graham loved it as she immediately started to act drunk as she moved around, tried to gently pull him away and more.

Graham started to walk East and he leant back a little as he started walking down a very, very steep slope down into a wooded valley below that might have once ran straight into the lake itself.

He was half way down when Bettie started drunk singing and pretending to dance.

He leant back a little more but he couldn't.

He fell forward and him and Bettie laughed together as they rolled down the hill.

Graham kissed Bettie's soft, beautiful lips as Fran, Harry and Sean ran down after them.

"It cannot be done," Graham said.

"I honestly wasn't even trying that hard to be drunk,"

"Do I need to take you to AA again?" Sean asked.

Graham laughed as Bettie playfully threw a handful of leaves at him. She had never been to AA and she hadn't drunk in months since becoming parents. Graham hadn't drunk in a month since a winery-related case.

"I doubt a man even as strong as Alex could have carried a drunk woman through a slopy woodland late at night with a drunk woman on his back. And come on, she would have had to be drunk to willingly go into the forest with him,"

Fran's phone buzzes. "This is what I've been waiting for. I've been running a social media scan again on all the photos, posts and footage done about the party, and one of the posts popped out,"

Graham was really glad Fran had decided to look at the posts instead of only the photos and videos.

"There was a single comment made about Alex White at the party, or actually two days before the party," Fran said. "The post reads *Watch Out Gals, Mr White Littedick is going. Don't let him touch you,*"

Graham shook his head as he got the jist that the woman writing that post was trying to warn the other girls at the party of what Alex was like.

"That confirms it then," Bettie said. "Sarah would have known what Alex was like so I cannot believe she would have gone willingly with him,"

Sean shook his head. "Definitely not but if we discount this location as the dumping ground for the bodies. Then where did he put them?"

Graham just grinned because that was a hell of a question and they were seriously running out of time to find out.

Alex always seemed to be ahead of them and maybe he was leaving little clues for them to chase in the wrong direction.

Graham looked at the woman he loved. "Where is Alex not wanting us to look?"

CHAPTER 12
18th October 2023
Canterbury, England
13:30

As much as Bettie wanted to just storm over to the south of the lake and examine the woodlands there, she really couldn't help but feel like they were missing something critical and it was only when Graham mentioned how Alex was trying to misdirect them that she realised what they were missing.

They were missing the other locations Alex had tried to lure the police too.

Bettie led the others back up the massive slope back to the SUV as Sean and Harry and Fran took out their phones and laptops and started searching for all the other locations the police had been searching and why.

Bettie took out her own phone and looked up Alex White a little more because she wanted to understand his past a little, and his education history even more.

She already knew he had been a university student two years ago and he had graduated, but she hadn't known that Alex had graduated with an immense score of 88/100.

Bettie couldn't believe that. That was an extreme score that just defied all logic, she didn't know a single person who had gotten that sort of score back in her university days. Alex was clearly as smart as they came.

But that was academic, book and research smart. It didn't always mean that Alex was real-world smart and that extreme score probably meant he was arrogant as hell.

"Just as you suspected auntie," Sean said.

Bettie gently took his phone off him and she smiled as she noticed that the police had all received notifications, tip-offs and funding from mysterious shell companies to support investigation efforts in the North and East of the lake.

"But nothing in the south or west," Graham said.

She still absolutely hated herself for getting him suspended but she could deal with that later, right now she really wanted to make progress on the case.

"What's exactly south-west of the lake?" Bettie asked.

Harry stepped forward showing her his laptop.

"Wow," Bettie said as she looked at a very small wooden hut that was almost invisible through the thick oak branches that covered the woodland.

"Let's go," Graham said.

Bettie shook her head. "Wait. Remember how smart Alex is, what if he planned for something like this? Let's find out a little more before we go crashing in there,"

Fran opened the SUV's door. "Can we at least research as we drive?"

Bettie nodded and boarded the massive SUV as Fran started driving off.

Bettie allowed the cold softness of the fake-leather SUV seating to claim her weight and she looked at Sean, Harry and Graham as they sat around her.

"The hut isn't registered on any database and it doesn't draw main power or water," Graham said.

"Auntie, there was once a police callout to the hut three years ago because a young man called the police about the smell of dead people inside,"

Bettie leant forward. The young man might have been Alex but if this was his secret lair then why would he call out the police?

Graham smiled. "The police conducted a full search of the area, they only sent two police officers and they found nothing. The report was buried as a prank but here's the kicker, two weeks later the cops disappeared,"

"He was studying police movements," Bettie said.

Everyone gasped in the SUV and Bettie couldn't believe Alex was so damn smart about all of this. She knew that Alex was all about studying and making sure he knew exactly what he was doing so it made sense for him to call out the police to see how they would react and search the area.

"The two officers were never found and the police still have two missing persons files open on them," Sean said.

The SUV jerked as Fran ran over a pothole.

"Okay," Bettie said. "I suspect Alex will have a bunch of cameras in the area so he could study the police. Sean, is it possible to find the feeds and cut them?"

"Sure," Sean said looking at Harry. "Give us a minute,"

Bettie loved watching their fingers dance over the keyboards of the laptops as they did computer magic she didn't understand.

As much as Bettie wanted to have back-up with them going after a serial killer, there wasn't the time nor resources. It annoyed Bettie more than she wanted to admit that the police weren't going to help so they were going in alone.

"We're one minute out," Fran said.

"I can kill the feed as soon as you say and it will lock him out forever," Sean said.

Bettie nodded. They were finally making progress but she didn't have the heart to tell her family that once the feed was killed he was going to know what was happening.

And then he might even come for them.

Something that terrified Bettie a lot more than she ever wanted to admit.

CHAPTER 13
18th October 2023
Canterbury, England
13:43

Alex was really looking forward to his flight on his private plane as he sat on a cold metal chair on Canterbury high street with a boiling hot mug of black bitter coffee in front of him.

There were so many female students just walking up and down the long cobblestone high street in their long, tight-fitting jeans, blouses and jumpers. Alex would have liked to know what the sweet women looked like underneath all those foul clothes but he couldn't do that anymore.

He had to focus on his mission to escape because there was a small chance that some idiot detective might have a break in the case. Of course no one was as smart as him so he doubted it.

But England was boring nowadays. All the English women screamed the same, flirted the same and died the same way.

But the US was the land of opportunity and there were millions of more young women to kill compared to the UK. The US was the definition of fertile hunting grounds.

His phone buzzed.

Alex took out his phone and smiled as he saw he could no longer access the security cameras around his home in the woods. That was strange and interesting and rather fascinating.

He normally only got contacted if some pretty young women had stumbled upon his lair but now someone had cut the feeds entirely.

It certainly wasn't the police because they weren't smart enough to find his home so that was more interesting.

Alex knew there was a new player in the game and hopefully it was a nice pretty woman.

Alex downed the boiling hot coffee in one as he scorched his throat and he just laughed. He had to go home and he had to see for himself who the new player was.

And if the player was a woman then regardless of her age he was going to enjoy killing her.

A final kill before the English lost him forever.

CHAPTER 14
18th October 2023
Canterbury, England
13:44

As Bettie stepped out of the SUV, the

blanket of dead leaves covering the woodland floor crunched under her feet and the sweet aromas of nature, rot and damp filled the air. There might not have been any pollution here but Bettie still didn't like the strange tang of rotten meat that clung to her lung.

Thick oak trees with wild branches shooting out in all directions littered the ground and Bettie just stopped when she saw the large wooden cabin.

From the aerial photo that Sean had shown her earlier she had thought this was a small little thing that might have offered hunters or whoever a little bit of refuge in a snowstorm or whatever (as if England actually had the extreme weather for such things) but Bettie was surprised how massive the cabin actually was.

Thick trunks of oak trees formed the walls, there were no windows and the front door was made from iron. Bettie didn't understand why someone would build a wonderful log cabin only to put something that awful on the front of it.

It made little sense so Bettie went over to it. She felt the ground harden under her and when she brushed away the leaves, she saw the concrete stepping stones. So maybe the owners of this place had liked and respected this cabin once, and at least wanted it to look beautiful.

Now Bettie didn't like it. This cabin just felt menacing.

She watched the others go onto the cabin, they knocked on the front door and Bettie knew no one would answer. Instead she looked up into the oak trees and saw ten well-hidden cameras high up so she knew that Alex could have been watching them for sure.

Bettie didn't want to be here any longer than needed.

She took out her phone, looked up Commander Knight's phone number in the Federation database and called him.

It went straight to voicemail but Bettie would rather tell him where they were in case anything went wrong.

"Knight," Bettie said into the voicemail, "we've found a wooden hut southwest of the lake. This is where Alex has been killing and preparing his victims, we need support immediately. Get here as soon as you can,"

Bettie hung up and she really hoped that by the time (and if) Knight got here they would have something to show him.

Bettie went over to her family and smiled as she watched Graham's ass as he bent over to pick the lock on the front door. He really did have an amazing ass and she still had no idea about how to fix his suspension.

She really had to make some phone calls later. She had to save the man she love's job.

"And here we go," Graham said trying to open the door but he couldn't.

Bettie kissed him on the cheek as she knelt down and picked the lock within a few seconds.

"I loosened it for you," Graham said.

"Sure you did babe," Bettie said opening the door. "Jesus Christ!"

Bettie coughed and gagged as the extreme smell of death, corpses and rotting flesh filled the air as something was released from the cabin.

It smelt so bad and Bettie really hated that the damn smell of dead body was going to get into her clothes. The smell of death had to be one of the worse things she had ever experienced and it was impossible to wash off.

Bettie was so annoyed at that because she had only bought this outfit two weeks ago.

Maybe if she washed it and gave it to a homeless person then she might feel better.

"Who wants to go first?" Fran asked backing away.

Bettie laughed as her, Graham and Sean turned on the torches on their phones and went inside.

Bettie managed to find a light switch to her left so she turned it on but she really wished she hadn't. It was a slaughter shop in there.

The immense log walls were covered in naked photos of tens upon tens of young women and the wall to Bettie's right was covered in photos of the young woman's bodies as they were sleeping in death.

The floor was covered in dry sticky blood and Bettie almost wanted to vomit at the sickness of a huge wooden table in the middle of the log.

It was covered in the rotting remains of corpses. There were a few heads, a few legs and a few arms but it was the "special" female organs that really turned Bettie's stomach.

She dialled 999 and asked for the police.

"This is President Bettie English. Code 111. I need police at my location immediately," she said.

The Code 111 was an emergency code that all police operators were meant to know that she was an extremely important person that needed to be taken seriously.

"Code 111?" the operator asked. "Is this a prank or something?"

"Please you have to get to my location now. You need to tell the police that I've found the victims of Alex White,"

"Who?" the operator asked. "I know I only started yesterday but this is just a textbook prank case. Goodbye,"

Bettie just laughed as the dumb operator hung up and she just shook her head.

Bettie was about to call Zoey Quill but she heard a car pull up outside.

"He's here," Graham said as he slammed the door shut behind him.

Bettie immediately started taking photos as did Graham, Sean and Harry and sent them to the Federation.

Fran pushed her tiny body against the iron front door as if she was actually going to stop Alex from coming inside.

Bettie really really wanted the police to turn up and finally help her before everyone she loved died and all this evidence was gone forever.

CHAPTER 15
18th October 2023
Canterbury, England
13:59

Alex White was surprised as he got out of his large grey Jeep that someone actually had been smart to find the log cabin where he had killed, enjoyed and buried a lot of his victims. Of course the new players couldn't be that intelligent because he only saw a black SUV.

Only one.

There weren't any police cars about, there weren't any police sirens in the distance and there was nothing about to endanger him or his plans.

Alex had wondered if he should have left the events to play out but he couldn't resist a little look, peak or taste of the new player that might have been a woman. And it would hardly be a bad thing to add another woman to his tally before he fled.

Alex went over to the SUV and slashed all four of the tyres with a pocket knife that his father had gifted him as a well done on his first kill when he was ten.

At least the new player couldn't escape and that meant they were never going to be able to stop him, his plans and the victims would never get justice. Because the victims didn't deserve justice or peace or anything.

As Alex went over to the iron front door, he could see that other people had been here and at least he got to kill more and more people instead of their leader. That was going to be fun.

Alex couldn't understand why people believed his victims were innocent. They were young slutty women wearing clothes far too short for their own good. Alex was a hero, he was reminding women why they needed to wear sensible clothes and not like porn stars.

Alex really didn't understand what this modern world had turned into and he was grateful that his father had taught him how the way had to be and how killing young slutty women was an act of kindness.

It was all about teaching women to be more respectful, conservative and righteous in their clothing choices.

And as Alex took out the cold metal key to the log cabin he was so looking forward to teaching even more people his lessons.

If only his father was here to see how much he was doing to make him proud.

CHAPTER 16
18th October 2023
Canterbury, England
14:00

Graham's heart leapt into his throat as he heard the lock of the massive iron door start to turn slowly. He looked around for a little knife, saw or just something this monster would have used for hacking up of the bodies.

But there was nothing.

Graham clicked his fingers and everyone grabbed the huge table covered in body parts and they all moved the table over to the metal door.

Then the locks stopped turning and Graham called Zoey Quill, he really hoped she was going to answer on the first ring.

She answered on the third. "What you got for me?"

"Southwest by the lake there's a cabin. Get units there now," Graham said. "And-"

Graham just looked at beautiful Bettie as he realised the phone call hadn't ended naturally. There was no phone service here all of a sudden and that meant Alex White probably had a phone jammer.

He really had thought of everything. Graham hardly would have been surprised if the monster had sliced the tires or something.

"We need to get out of here," Fran said.

Graham looked at Bettie. "Plan is you and me keep Alex busy. You three escape and run in completely different directions to get help,"

Everyone nodded and Graham just hugged Bettie. There was no way in hell he was allowing Alex to hurt her.

And as much as Graham wanted her to escape with the others. If anyone could stop Alex it would definitely be her.

The front door opened outwards.

Alex just laughed as he looked down at the table that was meant to stop him from getting in. Graham hadn't even realised what way the door opened when they had come in.

Graham just stared at Alex's posh, expensive business suit, crisp white shirt and polish black shoes. He looked like a movie star, not a serial killer.

Alex took out a pocketknife and looked at Bettie.

"You cannot get away with this," Graham said.

Alex smiled. "Get away with what? I have done nothing wrong. You cannot tie this place to me and even if you did I have the lawyers to get me out of this,"

Graham looked at Bettie as she was stretching and he couldn't help but focus on her breasts as much as he didn't want to.

Alex spat at her. "Disgusting slut. You're over thirty and still a monster lurking in weak-willed men and forcing yourself on them,"

Graham realised why Bettie was doing what she was and he noticed that on the table filled with body parts, all the "special" female parts were so carefully cut off that he supposed they had to be special to Alex for some reason.

Bettie grinned. "What happened to you then? What innocent woman lured you?"

Alex pointed the knife at Bettie. "Not me you slut. My father was a goodman, respected, a God Fearing man that loved his Church but then some slutty woman came into the Church, seduced him and forced herself on him,"

"Your mother?" Sean asked.

"Of course," Alex said, "when the slut revealed she was pregnant, my father did the right thing by marrying her, treating me with love and respect but God turned his back on him because he gave into temptation out of wedlock. My father lost everything because of that slut,"

"Intergenerational trauma," Bettie said.

Graham nodded. He had read recently how the trauma and hate and rage that the parents experienced could be passed onto the later generations so the father's trauma of losing everything he loved was passed onto Alex so he suffered exactly how his father did.

"Thankfully my father," Alex said, "killed the witch slut so he could be redeemed in God's eyes but it didn't work. So we kept killing and killing more sluts and demon worshippers just to make sure that one day God will forgive him,"

Graham really didn't have the heart to tell him that the bible did say that you only had to ask for forgiveness and God would do it. It was stupid considering that even people like Alex could find forgiveness and be cleansed of their sins despite of all the monstrous things he had done.

Alex jumped onto the table.

Graham and Bettie flew forward.

Grabbing the table.

Moving it to one side.

Alex laughed.

He flew at Bettie.

"Run!" Graham shouted.

Graham tackled Alex to the ground.

The three others ran out the door.

Alex headbutted Graham.

He didn't let go.

Alex rammed the pocketknife into Graham's arm.

He screamed.

Alex bit Graham's nose.

He released him.

Alex jumped up.

Kicking Graham in the stomach.

Then kicking Graham in the head.

And Graham's world went black.

CHAPTER 17
18th October 2023
Canterbury, England
14:17

As much as Sean absolutely hated leaving beautiful Harry and Fran by letting them run in different directions, he knew it was the right thing to do to save the auntie he loved. He had been running faster and faster along the long dirt road for close to twenty minutes now and he could hear something.

Or someone.

Sean was so glad him and Harry made each other stay in shape going to the gym together (for the cardio and other cute men more than anything else).

After running for another few moments around a corner he saw Commander Knight and Zoey Quill shouting about something in a massive clearing lined with oak trees and white-suited crime scene techs walked around them.

Acting clueless as usual.

As much as Sean hated the police with a passion because of everything they had put him and Harry through with the abuse and brain injury last year, he forced himself to run over to them.

"Zoey!" Sean shouted. "Auntie needs help. Alex has a knife. He's going to kill her,"

Zoey hugged him as soon as he reached them. Sean didn't want a hug but Zoey was a great hugger.

"He's lying," Commander Knight said.

"For God sake," Sean said. "Get your head out of your ass and help my auntie,"

Knight shook his head. "I told her not to be investigating this matter. She would have still been in custody if that DI hadn't been stupid,"

Zoey looked furious. "I am taking *my* people down there,"

Sean loved it when Zoey used her authority.

"I am in charge of forensics of Kent Police all your crime scene techs belong to me so you can give them to me and I will save Bettie. Or I can simply go over your head,"

"The choice is yours," Sean said trying to look as menacing as he could but realising his wonderful pink highlights didn't always help his case.

"I have a lake to search. The bodies are here and then we will arrest Alex,"

Sean laughed and looked at Zoey. "I promise you Zoey Auntie is going to die,"

Zoey stormed over to her crime scene techs. "Everyone! We are leaving this crime scene and going to the real one. I am sending you coordinates to the cabin and we have to go immediately. Quickly!"

All the techs rushed around and stopped what they were doing.

Sean smiled at Knight. "You had your chance to be the hero,"

Knight gripped Sean's throat. "You're going to let a serial killer walk! You're going to get women killed. You are a fucking idiot,"

A rock smashed Knight over the back of the head and Knight went down and Harry and Fran quickly threw the rock away like it was nothing.

Sean just kissed the man he loved on the lips and took him by the hand as Zoey pulled up in her car for them to save Bettie.

Because Sean knew time was running out for everyone.

CHAPTER 18
18th October 2023
Canterbury, England
14:30

Bettie just looked in utter horror as the idiot Alex finished making sure that Graham was well and truly knocked out. She really focused on the cold pocketknife in his hand in case he dared to attack Graham. There was no way in hell she was allowing the father of her children to die today, or any day for that matter.

"I don't kill men," Alex said. "I leave that to you sluts,"

Bettie really wanted to escape, make Alex reveal something but she got the sense that she was missing something. Something small but also something important because as choking as the smell of rotting flesh was, she didn't see any corpses.

Or not enough corpses or body parts considering how many victims Alex had.

"What happened to Sarah Hill?" Bettie asked.

Alex laughed. "As much as I would love to stay and chat I have a plane to catch and as you know you cannot charge me with anything. It is your word against mine,"

Bettie gasped as Alex pointed the pocketknife at her as he went out the front door and locked it firmly behind him.

Bettie was almost tempted to run over to the door, pound on it or something but there was no point. Alex would have been gone and he wasn't going to open it for her.

His only focus was on escaping now and she really needed to stop him.

Bettie went over to sexy Graham as he laid on the ground unconscious like he was sleeping. She really hoped the others would get help before 4 pm, but whilst Graham slept she needed to make sure she was searching for the evidence the police needed.

She went over to the body parts on the table and forced herself to study them. She hated the slimy feeling of one of the rotten arms she picked up but she understood that it was from one of the victims.

There was a tattoo on the shoulder of a raven. Bettie had seen that earlier as she went through the case files trying to understand who and why Alex killed.

His victim was Anna Carlisle, a young woman that disappeared three months ago after attending a party were Alex was. At least her family could get some closure.

Bettie looked at a very sticky and slimy and rotten ear that was on the table. It was small, a little deformed and Bettie nodded as she realised she had read about this in a newspaper nine months ago.

A young woman, barely 18, had disappeared one night walking home from sixth form. Amelia King had had an earring ripped out of her ear a few months before by a girl at school and she had ripped some of the flesh.

Bettie couldn't believe she had found at least two of the victims.

She looked at another one of the rotting arms on the table and she was surprised this one was preserved. The skin felt leathery and Bettie could have sworn little flecks of salt were falling off it.

The arm was still rotting but it was happening a lot slower.

Bettie realised this was the right leg and she knew exactly what Isabella had said only a few hours ago, there were fractures on the right leg.

As much as Bettie didn't want to do it, Zoey Quill had taught her how to forensically slice off flesh in an emergency.

After Bettie did that she just frowned and bit her lower lip as she realised she was holding the right leg of Sarah Hill. This was proof that she was dead and Alex had killed her.

But unless someone freed her shortly then the evidence was going to be useless.

The loud roar of flames told Bettie everything she needed to know.

Unless help arrived very, very quickly her, Graham and the evidence they needed were all going up in smoke.

Not exactly how Bettie wanted to die.

CHAPTER 19
18th October 2023
Canterbury, England
14:45

Alex White held a heavy cold metal container filled with petrol in his right hand as he looked at the log cabin that he had come to enjoy so much. He had already covered the SUV in petrol and he did want to light it up but he was annoyed by the entire situation.

He had no idea that Bettie English was investigating. He had read about her in the newspapers enough times to know that she could have been a threat to him, his freedom and his life's work.

For the sake of freeing mankind from the slutty predators of the world, he had to escape to the US and start his journey of freeing men from their predations.

Alex went over to the log cabin and started sloshing the rich petrol over the wood. He enjoyed the good smell of the petrol as it splashed against the wood.

It was such a shame that Bettie was going to burn alive. It was a waste of a life that shouldn't have ended because Bettie wasn't a slut and a real man like Graham shouldn't have to die either.

But it was evil sluts that were making him kill innocent people. If the sluts weren't about then he wouldn't have to do this.

Alex finished pouring the petrol on the cabin in front of the door so there would be extra fire there, making it impossible to escape and finally Bettie English would be dead so she could no longer stalk him and his so-called illegal activities.

He took out a lighter and lit the petrol. The fire roared to life and Alex didn't dare waste any time he had to make sure he was safe so he could continue his father's and the Lord's work.

He went over to the SUV and was about to light it up when he heard police sirens in the distance.

The foolish gays and the old woman had found someone to help them. Interesting.

He had already slashed the tyres so the SUV couldn't stop him so Alex simply went over to his own Jeep and drove away.

The police and the gays and that old woman would have a choice to make.

Stop him escaping or save Bettie English.

Alex just laughed as he knew he was well and truly safe.

CHAPTER 20
18th October 2023
Canterbury, England
14:50

Graham jumped up as soon as he heard the crackling, roaring, howling of the bright flames as he woke up. The choking toxic scent of burning flesh and wood and chemicals filled the air.

He pulled his hoody over his nose and went over to Bettie who was doing the same as she pounded on the log walls.

He kicked the walls harder and harder but they didn't move. They were made out of solid logs so they were impossible.

Graham looked around for a weak spot but chunks of the roof collapsed lighting up the table in the middle of the cabin.

Graham ran backwards against a very warm, sappy log wall and he really wanted to get out of here.

The thick black smoke burnt his eyes, his throat ached and his lungs started to protest more and more as the smoke started to invade.

He coughed again and again.

He couldn't even see Bettie through the darkness of the smoke.

Something collapsed overhead.

Graham jumped forward.

Another piece of wood smashed where he had been standing only moments ago.

When he landed on the ground his left hand went through the wooden floor and he felt a small bag.

He grabbed it as he swore he could have heard random voices through the flames but it could have just been his own mind playing cruel tricks on him.

A woman's hands grabbed him, throwing him over her shoulder and Graham gripped the bag tight as he was taken out of the building.

A moment later the woman fell and Graham was so glad to land on the hard leave-covered ground just watching the immense log cabin go up in flames, their evidence with it.

Graham smiled and kissed the woman he loved as Bettie just looked at him. And then Sean, Harry, Fran and plenty more people rushed over to them as a fire truck raced down to start putting out the fire.

"You can't get rid of me that easily," Graham said hugging Bettie tight. "Thanks for saving me,"

Bettie kissed him again. "I think you've saved this case,"

"What's in the bag?" Zoey asked.

Graham had never been so damn happy to see cute Zoey in her fit white lab coat in all his life.

He looked down at the small black canvas bag in his hand and he opened it revealing all sorts of bloodied instruments that were perfect for cutting up bodies like those on the middle table in the cabin.

And Graham noticed one of the knives in the bag had a very fresh and firm fingerprint on it in dry blood.

"Zoey," Graham said standing up, "we need to go to the nearest Federation contractor lab. Run these prints and start examining these things,"

Zoey took the bag and Graham waved over a police constable to go with her to maintain chain of custody given how desperate the situation was.

"Fran," Bettie said, "drive them please. I know Fiona always wants more Federation business and her labs should be empty enough for us to start straight away,"

Fran, Zoey and the constable ran away and Graham really hoped the fingerprints were a match to Alex because they were really running out of time.

"Auntie," Sean said, "we might have a small problem about Knight,"

"Sean English and Harry!" Knight shouted.

Graham just smiled at his nephew as a very angry Knight stormed towards them as he jumped out of a still-moving police car. Graham was really impressed at how stupid, pathetic and determined Knight was being.

The sooner Knight was gone, the sooner Graham would be happy.

"You assaulted a police officer," Knight said as he held his head.

Bettie couldn't believe this idiot and she was really starting to have enough of his stupidity.

"Really?" Graham asked. "I didn't see that. Are there any witnesses?"

Knight frowned. "Your nephews know exactly what happened and they committed a crime,"

"For fuck sake," Bettie said. "I don't have time for this. With me everyone,"

Graham simply followed the woman he loved as she led them all away from Knight.

Sean and Harry just grinned at each other and Graham really had to admit they were amazing and he did love them both.

"If what Graham found did turn out to be the evidence we need to convict Alex of murder coupled with what I found with the body parts that we might still be able to use despite the fire damage, I want to say that it is enough but I feel like something is missing,"

Graham completely agreed. "My problem is I want to know more about the murders themselves and how he did that,"

"Especially as Sarah Hill would have been dragged or carried a good few miles from the mansion to the house," Sean said.

"He had help," Bettie said grinning.

Graham gasped. Of course Alex had help because if every woman was on high alert about Alex they would have been watching each other like hawks to make sure no one went off with Alex.

Alex never could have gotten her out of the mansion the night of the party without help.

"Who would have helped him?" Harry asked.

Graham took out his phone and he liked it how Bettie stood really, really close to him. She smelt of smoke but she was still wonderful.

Graham cross-referenced every single suspect in all the sexual assault cases where Alex had been the prime suspect and only a single name popped up.

"Who's Jasmin Holt?" Graham asked.

Bettie looked up the name. "That's interesting. She's actually Alex's foster sister for a space of two years before she went missing and resurfaced past the age of 18 so Social Services weren't too bothered about the resurface. Not with budget cuts and minors in the system they had to deal with,"

Graham nodded. "So Alex gets his foster sister to help him? Why?"

Sean hissed and shook his head. "The answer is a lot simpler than you can imagine. Foster children aren't bad people in the slightest, they are simply children who were dealt a bad hand in life and they want love and family and safety,"

"Exactly," Harry said, "so when they go into a household with someone as controlling, evil and predatory as Alex. I don't doubt for a minute she was abused in that house so the parents never knew a thing and he forced her to do things for her own safety,"

Graham hated Alex even more. If he was a violent man, which he wasn't, he honestly might have killed the monster in revenge. Did his evil know no bounds?

"We have to find Jasmin now," Graham said.

Little did he know just how twisted this case was about to get.

CHAPTER 21
18th October 2023
Canterbury, England
15:45

Graham seriously hated it as he watched the constables drag in Jasmin into the police interview room. He hated how they were wasting so much time, she had been impossible to find and she had run away from the cops three times. She was a nightmare and Graham really, really hoped this was going to be useful.

Even more so with Fran confirming Alex had already boarded his private plane that was preparing to take him off to the US.

Graham just watched as the short little young woman in her black jeans, hoody and trainers struggled as the constable made her sit down.

Graham wasn't a fan of the grey walls, metal chair and horrible one-way mirror of the interview room but he didn't care too much about the location right now. He needed answers so a serial killer was about to walk away for murder.

He was only allowed in here because Bettie had twisted Knight's arm (hopefully not literally) to make him allow Graham to be back on official duty for this interview alone.

Now he needed to make it count.

"Your foster brother is a serial killer and predator," Graham said. "We know you helped him with the crimes. Tell us what happened and we can cut you a deal,"

Jasmin smiled like this was all some game.

"Come on Jasmin. We have found the DNA profiles of over ten women on his tools," Graham said really grateful Zoey had finished the lab tests two minutes ago. "You are going down for murder,"

Jasmin shook her head.

"If you don't believe me then convince me this wasn't murder," Graham said just hoping for something.

"It isn't murder silly detective. Me and my God are saving these women," Jasmin said. "All these women are the devil you know,"

Graham leant back as he saw something deranged in Jasmin's eyes. A hunger maybe, a lust for killing, or maybe something else entirely.

"These women are the monsters on this planet. God did not create women, everyone thinks they did but they are wrong. The Demon put women on this planet to corrupt innocent good men,"

Graham shook his head. "Why did you kill

them?"

Jasmin cocked her head and laughed manically.

"We didn't kill them. We freed them."

"How did you kill them?"

"We. Did. Not. Kill. Them!" Jasmin shouted as loud as she could.

Graham looked at his watch they only had ten minutes left. He needed to make Jasmin confess that Alex was a part of it.

"Was Alex White a part of this freeing?" Graham asked.

"Who? Only my God is a part of it,"

"What is your God called?"

"God obviously. You are such a silly detective,"

Graham smashed his fists onto the metal table and he took out his phone and showed Jasmin a picture of Alex White.

"Is this your God?"

Jasmin just grinned. "You're funny,"

He needed a confession, he needed evidence, he needed something to make sure he could lock up Alex for a long time.

As much as Graham loved the forensic proof that Zoey had found he knew it wasn't enough not unless something could say that Alex had killed each and every one of the victims.

And explained how he got the women to the locations.

Jasmin touched Graham's hand. "Join us. You could become the most powerful man in society if you simply wipe out us interior beings. Kill women to free *man*kind,"

Graham slapped the woman's hand away.

Bettie stormed into the interview room and slammed a laptop on the table. Graham realised she was showing them a satellite feed of the private airstrip where Alex was taking off from.

"This is a top-secret operation the Federation is watching thanks to our contacts in the CIA. They don't want Alex White on US soil so they will kill him at 4 pm,"

Jasmin frowned.

"If you don't tell me what I want to know the police cannot grab him and save him from certain death," Bettie said. "Do you understand me?"

Jasmin smiled as she watched the private plane start to taxi along the runway.

Graham had no idea how to get through to a crazy woman like Jasmin.

"You want safety, love and family?" Graham asked.

Jasmin looked at him.

"If Alex dies then who will protect you? Who will love you? Who will be your family?"

Jasmin's eyes started to turn wet and Bettie turned on the audio and Graham could have sworn Sean's voice was on the laptop.

"Alpha this is bravo. I have a clean shot. Do I have a green light?" Sean asked.

Graham forced himself not to laugh. He knew the police couldn't lie to a suspect in the UK but the Federation wasn't police.

"Green light," Harry said over the laptop. "Green light,"

"No!" Jasmin shouted. "Alex killed them, he did everything you know. Just save him. Just save my brother please,"

Bettie took out her phone. "Commander Knight this is Bettie English you have your evidence. Arrest the bastard,"

Graham just grinned as he watched armed police units swarm the private plane as he listened to Jasmin's crying as she probably realised either Alex was going to kill her or she had just betrayed him.

He wasn't going to let anything bad happen to her but Graham just couldn't understand how this had all happened in the first place.

But whatever happened next, Graham was more than glad he had been a part of it, getting a chance to solve a crime with the woman and family he loved, he got justice for tons of victims and he was finally going to understand what the hell had happened to the tragic case of Sarah Hill.

CHAPTER 22
18th October 2023
Canterbury, England
20:00

As Bettie sat on her wonderfully large black sofa with her little two sleeping angels in her arms, she couldn't deny how brilliant today had been and now it was even better because she was home with the family she loved more than anything.

The TV was off and Sean and Harry were just flipping through their phones and Harry rested his head on Sean's lap on the black sofa adjacent to hers.

She really did love times like this because these were the moments when they were simply a family. A normal loving family that didn't solve crimes, weren't millionaires (granted she was the only millionaire here) and they weren't anything else except a family.

Little Harrison and Elizabeth quietly snored away to themselves and occasionally woke up, looked at Bettie and then immediately fell back to sleep. They really were the cutest kids in the entire world.

They had only just got back from the police station and picking up the kids from her mother's so Bettie had fed the kids briefly and then just sat down with them whilst beautiful, sexy Graham was cooking dinner.

The rich aromas of tomato, garlic and sausages filled the air and Bettie was seriously looking forward to a great dinner. Graham had wanted to go foraging for mushrooms for dinner but Bettie had shot down that idea as soon as she could.

She might have loved Graham but he was useless at reading things from that app. And considering Graham would most probably pick up the deadly mushrooms she just wasn't risking it, no matter how much she loved him.

Her life was more important.

"What happened Auntie in the end?" Sean asked.

Bettie laughed as she told them about everything that had happened.

Back in the police station, Bettie and Graham had waited a good half an hour before a very grumpy Commander Knight stormed back with Alex in handcuffs and Bettie went behind the one-way mirror so her and Graham could watch what was about to go down.

There was an awful smell of sweat but Bettie just focused as Alex sat down and looked like he owned the place.

Then Commander Knight explained all the evidence they had against him and even that Jasmin had turned Crown Witness for them, something Bettie didn't even know at the time.

Bettie had loved it how shocked Alex looked and he knew he was done for so he looked straight at Bettie. She didn't know how he knew where she was but she knew he was looking at her and he wanted to kill her.

It was that simple.

Alex explained that he had recruited stupid Jasmin on the first time of her coming into their home where he had *enjoyed* her and threatened to kill her again and again if she ever told his parents about what he was doing.

When he realised how easy she was to manipulate and how desperate she was to stay in a loving home (because Alex's parents worshipped the ground they both walked on), Alex started to use it against her to bring him girls and force her to watch.

Over time Jasmin started to have less and less of a reaction to it all (Bettie had no idea how that was even possible) so Alex started doing what he was doing to the other girls on her to make sure she was still scared of him.

Then on the night of the party, Jasmin had lured Sarah Hill upstairs because she wanted to tell Sarah a secret about Alex, and Sarah, always the person wanting to help out a fellow woman in trouble, fell into her trap.

As soon as Sarah walked into the door, Alex knocked her out and *enjoyed* her a little bit before knocking her out and Jasmin folded up the body into a sports-bags with empty bottles of alcohol popping out of the bag.

Bettie liked that little touch. No one would bat an eyelid to someone getting rid of empty bottles not when there were so many drinks, drugs and sex to enjoy as the night went on.

Jasmin went into her car and did the long drive towards the cabin where Alex had already hiked and then he simply did what he did best.

"And that's what happened," Bettie said as little Elizabeth woke up and looked like she was about to kiss Bettie before she went back to sleep.

"This was all a case of a random woman just dying because she was lured into a trap?" Harry asked. "This wasn't personal or had any sense of twisted logic,"

Bettie nodded. She understood what they meant, normally a killer had some sort of twisted logic for their crimes but he didn't. Alex White was just an abusive monster that was thankfully never ever going to see the light of day again.

"Then why," Harry said sitting up and accidentally crushing one of Sean's balls if his face was to be believed, "did Alex tell his cellmate about the lake and what did the police know?"

Bettie laughed. "If I've learnt anything about Alex White, it is that he likes a challenge, he likes to believe he is cunning and I believe he told his cellmate about the lake just to see what would happen. And if anyone was smart enough to catch him,"

"Well you were," Graham said. "Dinner should be done in a few minutes,"

As soon as the words about food had left Graham's wonderful mouth both the kids woke up and looked at Graham. Bettie laughed and kissed them both.

"And no," Bettie said, "I think Knight is just as silly as the rest of the top-brass. I don't think he ever knew what he was looking for,"

Graham sighed as he sat down on the floor by Bettie's feet like he always did when he was sad or something.

"Commander Knight is the lead on my Conduct Hearing that is scheduled to start in three weeks' time," Graham said.

"Shit," Bettie said, "how could they actually go through with the Police Conduct

Hearing? You're the finest officer they have,"

"When you refuse to turn a blind eye to all the racism, homophobia and corruption in the police, you have tons of enemies over the years. I know this year has only added to my list of enemies,"

Bettie couldn't deny that.

A timer went off in the kitchen and Graham, Harry and Sean all went off into the kitchen to help serve up dinner. Bettie pulled her little angels tight and she was so pleased that her and the team had put another killer behind bars, gotten victims a lot of justice and finally solved the case of Sarah Hill so Isabella could get some peace at least.

And whilst Graham's conduct hearing was a massive cause for concern that was a problem for next month but Bettie would be prepared, because no one came after her boyfriend and lived to tell the tale.

Next month she was going on a war footing and she wasn't taking any prisoners at all.

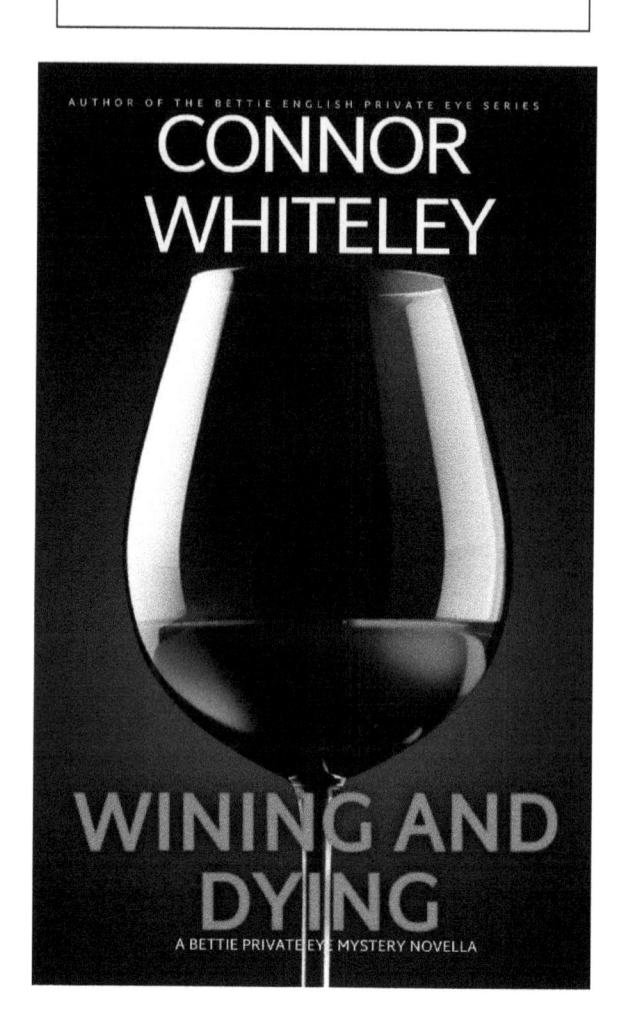

Sign Up Bonus

Keep up to date with exclusive deals on Connor Whiteley's Books, as well as the latest news about new releases and so much more!

Sign up for the Grab a Book and Chill Monthly newsletter, and you'll get one **FREE** ebook just for signing up: Agents of The Emperor Collection.

Sign Up Now!

https://dl.bookfunnel.com/f4p5xkprbk

Subscriptions:

Never miss an issue!

3 Month Subscription… $14.99

6 Month Subscription… $29.99

12 Month Subscription… $49.99

Subscribe Up Now!

https://payhip.com/b/aMJyj